A DAUGHTER OF THE DONS

A Story of New Mexico Today

WILLIAM MACLEOD RAINE

1ˢᵗ WORLD
LIBRARY
Literary Society

A Daughter of the Dons

William MacLeod Raine

© 1st World Library, 2008
PO Box 2211
Fairfield, IA 52556
www.1stworldlibrary.com
First Edition

LCCN: 2007940235

Softcover ISBN: 978-1-4218-9372-3
Hardcover ISBN: 978-1-4218-9472-0
eBook ISBN: 978-1-4218-9272-6

Purchase *"A Daughter of the Dons"*
as a traditional bound book at:
www.1stWorldLibrary.com/purchase.asp?ISBN=978-1-4218-9372-3

1st World Library is a literary, educational organization
dedicated to:

- Creating a free internet library of downloadable ebooks

- Hosting writing competitions and offering book publishing
  scholarships.

Interested in more 1st World Library books? contact:
literacy@1stworldlibrary.com
Check us out at: www.1stworldlibrary.com

1st World Library Literary Society

Giving Back to the World

"If you want to work on the core problem, it's early school literacy."

- James Barksdale, former CEO of Netscape

"No skill is more crucial to the future of a child, or to a democratic and prosperous society, than literacy."

- Los Angeles Times

"Literacy... means far more than learning how to read and write... The aim is to transmit... knowledge and promote social participation."

- UNESCO

"Literacy is not a luxury, it is a right and a responsibility. If our world is to meet the challenges of the twenty-first century we must harness the energy and creativity of all our citizens."

- President Bill Clinton

"Parents should be encouraged to read to their children, and teachers should be equipped with all available techniques for teaching literacy, so the varying needs and capacities of individual kids can be taken into account."

- Hugh Mackay

CONTENTS

I. DON MANUEL INTRODUCES HIMSELF.........................7

II. THE TWO GRANTS 15

III. FISHERMAN'S LUCK 25

IV. AT THE YUSTE HACIENDA 39

V. "AN OPTIMISTIC GUY" 55

VI. JUANITA..67

VII. TWO MESSAGES 78

VIII. TAMING AN OUTLAW 89

IX. OF DON MANUEL AND MOONLIGHT 98

X. MR. AINSA DELIVERS A MESSAGE 109

XI. THE SIXTEENTH CENTURY AND
THE TWENTIETH.. 122

XII. "I BELIEVE YOU'RE IN LOVE WITH HER TOO" ... 131

XIII. AMBUSHED 139

XIV. MANUEL TO THE RESCUE 150

XV. ONE THOUSAND DOLLARS REWARD 167

XVI. VALENCIA MAKES A PROMISE 174

XVII. AN OBSTINATE MAN 184

XVIII. MANUEL INTERFERES 198

XIX. VALENCIA ACCEPTS A RING 206

XX. DICK LIGHTS A CIGARETTE 211

XXI. WHEN THE WIRES WERE CUT 222

XXII. THE ATTACK 231

XXIII. THE TIN BOX 246

XXIV. DICK GORDON APOLOGIZES 256

XXV. THE PRINCE CONSORT............................ 264

CHAPTER I

DON MANUEL INTRODUCES HIMSELF

For hours Manuel Pesquiera had been rolling up the roof of the continent in an observation-car of the "Short Line."

His train had wound in and out through a maze of bewildering scenery, and was at last dipping down into the basin of the famous gold camp.

The alert black eyes of the young New Mexican wandered discontentedly over the raw ugliness of the camp. Towns straggled here and there untidily at haphazard, mushroom growths of a day born of a lucky "strike." Into the valleys and up and down the hillsides ran a network of rails for trolley and steam cars. Everywhere were the open tunnel mouths or the frame shaft-houses perched above the gray Titan dump beards.

The magic that had wonderfully brought all these manifold activities into being had its talisman in the word "Gold"; but, since Pesquiera had come neither as a prospector nor investor, he heard with only half-concealed impatience the easy gossip of his fellow travelers about the famous ore producers of the district.

It was not until his inattentive ears caught the name of Dick Gordon that he found interest in the conversation.

"Pardon, sir! Are you acquaint' with Mr. Richard Gordon?" he asked, a touch of the gentle Spanish accent in his voice.

The man to whom he had spoken, a grizzled, weather-beaten little fellow in a corduroy suit and white, broad-brimmed felt hat, turned his steady blue eyes on his questioner a moment before he answered:

"I ought to know him, seeing as I'm his partner."

"Then you can tell me where I may find him?"

"Yes, sir, I can do that. See that streak of red there on the hill—the one above the big dump. That's the shafthouse of the Last Dollar. Drop down it about nine hundred feet and strike an airline west by north for about a quarter of a mile, and you'd be right close to him. He's down there, tackling a mighty uncertain proposition. The shaft and the workings of the Last Dollar are full of water. He's running a crosscut from an upraise in the Radley drift, so as to tap the west tunnel of the Last Dollar."

"It is dangerous, you inform me?"

"Dangerous ain't the word. It's suicide, the way I look at it. See here, my friend. His drill goes through and lets loose about 'steen million gallons of water. How is he going to get in out of the rain about that time?"

The New Mexican showed a double row of pearly teeth in a bland smile.

"Pardon, sir. If you would explain a leetle more fully I would then comprehend."

"Sure. Here's the way it is. Dick and his three men are plugging away at the breast of the drift with air-drills. Every day he gits closeter to that lake dammed up there. Right now there can't be more'n a few feet of granite 'twixt him and it. He don't know how many any more'n a rabbit, because he's going by old maps that ain't any too reliable. The question is whether the wall will hold till he dynamites it through, or whether the weight of water will crumple up that granite and come pouring out in a flood."

"Your friend, then, is in peril, is it not so?"

"You've said it. He's shooting dice with death. That's the way I size it up. If the wall holds till it's blown up, Dick has got to get back along the crosscut, lower himself down the upraise, and travel nearly a mile through tunnelings before he reaches a shaft to git out. That don't leave them any too much time at the best. But if the water breaks through on them, it's Heaven help Dick, and good-by to this world."

"Then Mr. Gordon is what you call brave?"

"He's the gamest man that ever walked into this camp. There ain't an inch of him that ain't clear grit through and through. Get into a tight place, and he's your one best bet to tie to."

"Mr. Gordon is fortunate in his friend," bowed the New Mexican politely.

The little miner looked at him with shining eyes.

"Nothing like that. Me, I figure the luck's all on my side. Onct you meet Dick you'll see why we boost for him. Hello, here's where we get off at. If you're looking for Dick, stranger, you better follow me. I'm going right up to the mine. Dick had ought to be coming up from below any minute now."

Pesquiera checked his suitcase at the depot newsstand and walked up a steep hill trail with his guide. The miner asked no questions of the New Mexican as to his business with Gordon, nor did the latter volunteer any information. They discussed instead the output of the camp for the preceding year, comparing it with that of the other famous gold districts of the world.

Just as they entered the shafthouse the cage shot to the surface. From it stepped two men.

Several miners crowded toward them with eager greetings, but they moved aside at sight of Pesquiera's companion, who made straight for those from below.

"What's new, Tregarth?" he asked of one of them, a huge Cornishman.

"The drill have brook into the Last Dollar tunnel. The watter of un do be leaking through, Measter Davis. The boss sent us oop while Tom and him stayed to put the charges in the drill holes to blow oot the wall. He wouldna coom and let me stay."

Davis thought a moment.

"I'll go down the shaft and wait at the foot of it. There'll be something doing soon. Keep your eye peeled for signals, Smith, and when you git the bell to raise, shoot her up sudden. If the water's coming, we'll be in a hurry, and don't you forget it. Want to come down with me, Tregarth?"

"I do that, sir." The man stepped into the cage and grinned.

William MacLeod Raine

"We'll bring the byes back all right. Bet un we do, lads."

The cage shot down, and the New Mexican sat on a bench to wait its return. Beside him was a young doctor, who had come prepared for a possible disaster. Such conversation as the men carried on was in low tones, for all felt the strain of the long minutes. The engineer's eye was glued to his machinery, his hand constantly on the lever.

It must have been an hour before the bell rang sharply in the silence and the lever swept back instantly. A dozen men started to their feet and waited tensely. Next moment there was a wild, exultant cheer.

For Tregarth had stepped from the cage with a limp figure in his arms, and after him Davis, his arm around the shoulder of a drenched, staggering youth, who had a bleeding cut across his cheek. Through all the grime that covered the wounded miner the pallor of exhaustion showed itself.

But beaten and buffeted as the man had plainly been in his fight for life, the clean, supple strength and the invincible courage of him still shone in his eye and trod in his bearing. It was even now the salient thing about him, though he had but come, alive and no more, from a wrestle with death itself.

He sank to a bench, and looked around on his friends with shining eyes.

"'Twas nip and tuck, boys. The water caught us in the tunnel, and I thought we were gone. It swept us right to the cage," he panted.

"She didn't sweep Tom there, boss; ye went back after un," corrected the Cornishman.

"Anyhow, we made it in the nick o' time. Tom all right, Doctor?"

The doctor looked up from his examination.

"No bones broken. He seems sound. If there are no internal injuries it will be a matter of only a day or two in bed."

"Good. That's the way to talk. You got to make him good as new, Doctor. You ought to have seen the way he stayed by that drill when the water was pouring through the cracks in the granite. Have him taken to the hospital, and send the bill to me."

Tregarth boomed out in a heavy bass:

"What's the matter with the boss? Both of un? They be all right. Bean't they, lads?"

It was just after the answering chorus that Pesquiera came forward and bowed magnificently to the young mine operator. The New Mexican's eyes were blazing with admiration, for he was of Castilian blood and cherished courage as the chief of virtues.

"I have the honor to salute a hero, *senor*" he cried enthusiastically. "Your deed is of a most fine bravery. I, Manuel Pesquiera, say it. Have I the right in thinking him of the name of Mr. Richard Gordon?"

Something that was almost disgust filmed the gray eyes of the young miner. He had the Anglo-Saxon horror of heroics. What he had done was all in the day's work, and he was the last man in the world to enjoy having a fuss made over it.

"My name is Gordon," he said quietly.

The Spaniard bowed again.

"I have the honor to be your servant to command, Don Manuel Pesquiera. I believe myself to be, sir, a messenger of fortune to you—a Mercury from the favoring gods, with news of good import. I, therefore, ask the honor of an audience at your convenience."

Dick flung the wet hat from his curly head and took a look at the card which the Spaniard had presented him. From it his humorous gaze went back to the posturing owner of the pasteboard. Suppressing a grin, he answered with perfect gravity.

"If you will happen round to the palace about noon to-morrow, *Senor* Pesquiera, you will be admitted to the presence by the court flunkies. When you're inquiring for the whereabouts of the palace, better call it room 14, Gold Nugget Rooming-House."

He excused himself and stepped lightly across to his companion in the adventure, who had by this time recovered consciousness.

"How goes it, Tom? Feel as if you'd been run through a sausage-grinder?" he asked cheerily.

The man smiled faintly. "I'm all right, boss. The boys tell me you went back and saved me."

"Sho! I just grabbed you and slung you in the cage. No trick at all, Tom. Now, don't you worry, boy. Just lie there in the hospital and rest easy. We're settling the bill, and there's a hundred plunks waiting you when you get well."

Tom's hand pressed his feebly.

"I always knew you were white, boss."

The doctor laughed as he came forward with a basin of water and bandages.

"I'm afraid he'll be whiter than he need be if I don't stop that bleeding. I think we're ready for it now, Mr. Gordon."

"All right. It's only a scratch," answered Gordon indifferently.

Pesquiera, feeling that he was out of the picture, departed in search of a hotel for the night. He was conscious of a strong admiration for this fair brown-faced Anglo-Saxon who faced death so lightly for one of his men. Whatever else he might prove to be, Richard Gordon was a man.

The New Mexican had an uneasy prescience that his mission was foredoomed to failure and that it might start currents destined to affect potently the lives of many in the Rio Chama Valley.

CHAPTER II

THE TWO GRANTS

The clock in the depot tower registered just twelve, and the noon whistles were blowing when Pesquiera knocked at apartment 14, of the Gold Nugget Rooming-House.

In answer to an invitation to "Come in," he entered an apartment which seemed to be a combination office and living-room. A door opened into what the New Mexican assumed to be a sleeping chamber, adjoining which was evidently a bath, judging from the sound of splashing water.

"With you in a minute," a voice from within assured the guest.

The splashing ceased. There was the sound of a towel in vigorous motion. This was followed by the rustling of garments as the bather dressed. In an astonishingly short time the owner of the rooms appeared in the doorway.

He was a well-set-up youth, broad of shoulder and compact of muscle. The ruddy bloom that beat through the tanned cheeks and the elasticity of his tread hinted at an age not great, but there was no suggestion of immaturity in the cool steadiness of the gaze or in the quiet poise of the attitude.

He indicated a chair, after relieving his visitor of hat and cane. Pesquiera glanced at the bandage round the head.

"I trust, *senor*, your experience of yesterday has not given you a wakeful night?"

"Slept like a top. Fact is, I'm just getting up. You heard this morning yet how Tom is?"

"The morning newspaper says he is doing very well indeed."

"That's good hearing. He's a first-rate boy, and I'd hate to hear worse of him. But I mustn't take your time over our affairs. I think you mentioned business, sir?"

The Castilian leaned forward and fixed his black, piercing eyes on the other. Straight into his business he plunged.

"Senor Gordon, have you ever heard of the Valdes grant?"

"Not to remember it. What kind of a grant is it?"

"It is a land grant, made by Governor Facundo Megares, of New Mexico, which territory was then a province of Spain, to Don Fernando Valdes, in consideration of services rendered the Spanish crown against the Indians."

Dick shook his head. "You've got me, sir. If I ever heard of it the thing has plumb slipped my mind. Ought I to know about it?"

"Have you ever heard of the Moreno grant?"

Somewhere in the back of the young man's mind a faint memory stirred. He seemed to see an old man seated at a table in a big room with a carved fireplace. The table was littered

William MacLeod Raine

with papers, and the old gentleman was explaining them to a woman. She was his daughter, Dick's mother. A slip of a youngster was playing about the room with two puppies. That little five-year-old was the young mine operator.

"I have," he answered calmly.

"You know, then, that a later governor of the territory, Manuel Armijo, illegally carved half a million acres out of the former grant and gave it to Jose Moreno, from whom your grandfather bought it."

The miner's face froze to impassivity. He was learning news. The very existence of such a grant was a surprise to him. His grandfather and his mother had been dead fifteen years. Somewhere in an old trunk back in Kentucky there was a tin box full of papers that might tell a story. But for the present he preferred to assume that he knew what information they contained.

"I object to the word illegal, Don Manuel," he answered curtly, not at all sure his objection had any foundation of law.

Pesquiera shrugged. "Very well, *senor*. The courts, I feel sure, will sustain my words."

"Perhaps, and perhaps not."

"The law is an expensive arbiter, Senor Gordon. Your claim is slight. The title has never been perfected by you. In fifteen years you have paid no taxes. Still your claim, though worthless in itself, operates as a cloud upon the title of my client, the Valdes heir."

Dick looked at him steadily and nodded. He began to see the

purpose of this visit. He waited silently, his mind very alert.

"*Senor*, I am here to ask of you a relinquishment. You are brave; no doubt, chivalrous—"

"I'm a business man, Don Manuel," interrupted Gordon. "I don't see what chivalry has got to do with it."

"Senorita Valdes is a woman, young and beautiful. This little estate is her sole possession. To fight for it in court is a hardship that Senor Gordon will not force upon her."

"So she's young and beautiful, is she?"

"The fairest daughter of Spain in all New Mexico," soared Don Manuel.

"You don't say. A regular case of beauty and the beast, ain't it?"

"As one of her friends, I ask of you not to oppose her lawful possession of this little vineyard."

"In the grape business, is she?"

"I speak, *senor*, in metaphor. The land is barren, of no value except for sheep grazing."

"Are you asking me to sell my title or give it?"

"It is a bagatelle—a mere nothing. The title is but waste paper, I do assure. Yet we would purchase—for a nominal figure—merely to save court expenses."

"I see," Dick laughed softly. "Just to save court expenses—because you'd rather I'd have the money than the lawyers.

That's right good of you."

Pesquiera talked with his hands and shoulders, sparkling into animation. "Mr. Gordon distrusts me. So? Am I not right? He perhaps mistakes me for what you call a—a pettifogger, is it not? I do assure to the contrary. The blood of the Pesquieras is of the bluest Castilian."

"Fine! I'll take your word for it, Don Manuel. And I don't distrust you at all. But here's the point. I'm a plain American business man. I don't buy and I don't sell without first investigating a proposition submitted to me. I'm from Missouri."

"Oh, indeed! From St. Louis perhaps. I went to school there when I was a boy."

Gordon laughed. "I was speaking in metaphor, Don Manuel. What I mean is that I'll have to be shown. No pig-in-a-poke business for me."

"Exactly. Most precisely. Have I not traveled from New Mexico up this steep roof of the continent merely to explain how matters stand? Valencia Valdes is the true and rightful heiress of the valley. She is everywhere so recognize' and accept' by the peons."

The miner's indolent eye rested casually upon his guest. "Married?"

"I have not that felicitation," replied the Spaniard.

"It was the lady I meant."

"Pardon. No man has yet been so fortunate to win the *senorita*"

"I reckon it's not for want of trying, since the heiress is so beautiful. There's always plenty of willing lads to take over the job of prince regent under such circumstances."

The spine of the New Mexican stiffened ever so slightly. "Senorita Valdes is princess of the Rio Chama valley. Her dependents understan' she is of a differen' caste, a descendant of the great and renowned Don Alvaro of Castile."

"Don't think I know the gentleman. Who was he?" asked Gordon genially, offering his guest a cigar.

Pesquiera threw up his neat little hands in despair. "But of a certainty Mr. Gordon has read of Don Alvaro de Valdes y Castillo, lord of demesnes without number, conqueror of the Moors and of the fierce island English who then infested Spain in swarms. His retinue was as that of a king. At his many manors fed daily thirty thousand men at arms. In all Europe no knight so brave, so chivalrous, so skillful with lance and sword. To the nobles his word was law. Young men worshiped him, the old admired, the poor blessed. The queen, it is said, love' him madly. She was of exceeding beauty, but Don Alvaro remember his vows of knighthood and turn his back upon madness. Then the king, jealous for that his great noble was better, braver and more popular than he, send for de Valdes to come to court."

"I reckon Don Alvaro ought to have been sick a-bed that day and unable to make the journey," suggested Dick.

"So say his wife and his men, but Don Alvaro scorn to believe his king a traitor. He kiss his wife and babies good-bye, ride into the trap prepare' for him, and die like a soldier. God rest his valiant soul."

"Some man. I'd like to have met him," Gordon commented.

"Senorita Valencia is of the same blood, of the same fine courage. She, too, is the idol of her people. Will Mr. Gordon, who is himself of the brave heart, make trouble for an unprotected child without father or mother?"

"Unprotected isn't quite the word so long as Don Manuel Pesquiera is her friend," the Coloradoan answered with a smile.

The dark young man flushed, but his eyes met those of Dick steadily. "You are right, sir. I stand between her and trouble if I can."

"Good. Glad you do."

"So I make you an offer. I ask you to relinquish your shadowy claim to the illegal Moreno grant."

"Well, I can't tell you offhand just what I'll do, Don Manuel. Make your proposition to me in writing, and one month from to-day I'll let you know whether it's yes or no."

"But the *senorita* wants to make improvements—to build, to fence. Delay is a hardship. Let us say a thousand dollars and make an end."

"Not if the court knows itself. You say she's young. A month's wait won't hurt her any. I want to look into it. Maybe you're offering me too much. A fifth of a cent an acre is a mighty high price for land. I don't want any fairest daughter of Spain to rob herself for me, you know," he grinned.

"I exceed my instructions. I offer two thousand, Mr. Gordon."

"If you said two hundred thousand, I'd still say no till I had looked it up. I'm not doing business to-day at any price, thank you."

"You are perhaps of an impression that this land is valuable. On the contrary, I offer an assurance. And our need of your shadowy claim—"

"I ain't burdened with impressions, except one, that I don't care to dispose of my ghost-title. We'll talk business a month from to-day, if you like. No sooner. Have a smoke, Don Manuel?"

Pesquiera declined the proffered cigar with an impatient gesture. He rose, reclaimed his hat and cane, and clicked his heels together in a stiff bow.

He was a slight, dark, graceful man, with small, neat hands and feet, trimly gloved and shod. He had a small black mustache pointing upward in parallels to his smooth, olive cheeks. The effect was almost foppish, but the fire in the snapping eyes contradicted any suggestion of effeminacy. His gaze yielded nothing even to the searching one of Gordon.

"It is, then, war between us, Senor Gordon?" he asked haughtily.

Dick laughed.

"Sho! It's just business. Maybe I'll take your offer. Maybe I won't. I might want to run down and look at the no-'count land," he said with a laugh.

"I think it fair to inform you, sir, that the feeling of the country down there is in favor of the Valdes grant. The peons are hot-tempered, and are likely to resent any attempt to change the existing conditions. Your presence, *senor*, would be a danger."

"Much obliged, Don Manuel. Tell 'em from me that I got a bad habit of wearing a six-gun, and that if they get to resenting too arduous it's likely to ventilate their enthusiasm."

Once more the New Mexican bowed stiffly before he retired.

Pesquiera had overplayed his hand. He had stirred in the miner an interest born of curiosity and a sense of romantic possibilities. Dick wanted to see this daughter of Castile who was still to the simple-hearted shepherds of the valley a princess of the blood royal. Don Manuel was very evidently her lover. Perhaps it was his imagination that had mixed the magic potion that lent an atmosphere of old-world pastoral charm to the story of the Valdes grant. Likely enough the girl would prove commonplace in a proud half-educated fashion that would be intolerable for a stranger.

But even without the help of the New Mexican the situation was one which called for a thorough personal investigation. Gordon was a hard-headed American business man, though he held within him the generous and hare-brained potentialities of a soldier of fortune. He meant to find out just what the Moreno grant was worth. After he had investigated his legal standing he would look over the valley of the Chama himself. He took no stock in Don Manuel's assurance that the land was worthless, any more than he gave weight to his warning that a personal visit to the scene would be dangerous if the settlers believed he came to interfere with their rights. For many turbulent years Dick Gordon had held his own in a frontier community where untamed enemies had passed him daily with hate in their hearts. He was not going to let the sulky resentment of a few shepherds interfere with his course now.

A message flashed back to a little town in Kentucky that afternoon. It was of the regulation ten-words length, and this was the body of it:

Send immediately, by express, little brown leather trunk in garret.

The signature at the bottom of it was "Richard Gordon."

CHAPTER III

FISHERMAN'S LUCK

A fisherman was whipping the stream of the Rio Chama.

In his creel were a dozen trout, for the speckled beauties had been rising to the fly that skipped across the top of the riffles as naturally as life. He wore waders, gray flannel shirt, and khaki coat. As he worked up the stream he was oftener in its swirling waters than on the shore. But just now the fish were no longer striking.

"Time to grub, anyhow. I'll give them a rest for a while. They'll likely be on the job again soon," he told himself as he waded ashore.

A draw here ran down to the river, and its sunny hillside tempted him to eat his lunch farther up.

Into the little basin in which he found himself the sun had poured shafts of glory to make a very paradise of color. Down by the riverside the willows were hesitating between green and bronze. Russet and brown and red peppered the slopes, but shades of yellow predominated in the gulch itself.

The angler ate his sandwiches leisurely, and stretched his

lithe body luxuriantly on the ground for a *siesta*. When he resumed his occupation the sun had considerably declined from the meridian. The fish were again biting, and he landed two in as many minutes.

The bed of the river had been growing steeper, and at the upper entrance of the little park he came to the first waterfall he had seen. Above this, on the opposite side, was a hole that looked inviting. He decided that a dead tree lying across the river would, at a pinch, serve for a bridge, and he ventured upon it. Beneath his feet the rotting bark gave way. He found himself falling, tried desperately to balance himself, and plunged head first into the river.

Coming to the surface, he caught at a rock which jutted from the channel. At this point the water was deep and the current swift. Were he to let loose of the boulder he must be swept over the fall before he could reach the shore. Nor could he long maintain his position against the rush of the ice-cold waters fresh from the mountain snow fields.

He had almost made up his mind to take his chances with the fall, when a clear cry came ringing to him:

"*No suelte!*"

A figure was flying down the slope toward him—the slim, graceful form of a woman. As she ran she caught up a stick from the ground. This she held out to him from the bank.

He shook his head.

"I would only drag you in."

She put her fingers to her mouth and gave a clear whistle. Far up on the slope a pony lifted its head and nickered.

Again her whistle shrilled, and the bronco trotted down toward her.

"Can you hold on?" she asked in English.

He was chilled to the marrow, but he answered quietly: "I reckon."

She was gone, swift-footed as a deer, to meet the descending animal. He saw her swing to the saddle and lean over it as the pace quickened to a gallop.

He did not know her fingers were busy preparing the rawhide lariat that depended from the side of the saddle. On the very bank she brought up with a jerk that dragged her mount together, and at the same moment slipped to the ground.

Running open the noose of the lariat, she dropped it surely over his shoulders. The other end of the rope was fastened to the saddle-horn, and the cow-pony, used to roping and throwing steers, braced itself with wide-planted front feet for the shock.

"Can you get your arm through the loop?" cried the girl.

His arms were like lead, and almost powerless. With one hand he knew he could not hang on. Nor did he try longer than for that one desperate instant when he shot his fist through the loop. The wall of water swept him away, but the taut rope swung him shoreward.

Little hands caught hold of him and fought with the strong current for the body of the almost unconscious man; fought steadily and strongly, for there was strength in the small wrists and compact muscle in the shapely arms. She was waist deep in the water before she won, for from above she could find no purchase for the lift.

The fisherman's opening eyes looked into dark anxious ones that gazed at him from beneath the longest lashes he had ever seen. He had an odd sense of being tangled up in them and being unable to escape, of being both abashed and happy in his imprisonment. What he thought was: "They don't have eyes like those out of heaven." What he said was entirely different.

"Near thing. Hadn't been for you I wouldn't have made it."

At his words she rose from her knees to her full height, and he saw that she was slenderly tall and fashioned of gracious curves. The darkness of her clear skin was emphasized by the mass of blue-black hair from which little ears peeped with exquisite daintiness. The mouth was sweet and candid, red-lipped, with perfect teeth just showing in the full arch. The straight nose, with its sensitive nostrils, proclaimed her pure patrician.

"You are wet," he cried. "You went in after me."

She looked down at her dripping skirts, and laughter rippled over her face like the wind in golden grain. It brought out two adorable dimples near the tucked-in corners of her mouth.

"I am damp," she conceded.

"Why did you do it? The water might have swept you away," he chided, coming to a sitting posture.

"And if I hadn't it might have swept you away," she answered, with a flash of her ivory teeth.

He rose and stood before her.

"You risked your life to save mine."

"Is it not worth it, sir?"

"That ain't for me to say. The point is, you took the chance."

Her laughter bubbled again. "You mean, I took the bath."

"I expect you'll have to listen to what I've got to say, ma'am."

"Are you going to scold me? Was I precipitate? Perhaps you were attempting suicide. Forgive, I pray."

He ignored her raillery, and told her what he thought of a courage so fine and ready. He permitted a smile to temper his praise, as he added: "You mustn't go jumping in the river after strangers if you don't want them to say, 'Thank you kindly.' You find four out of five of them want to, don't you?"

"It is not yet a habit of mine. You're the first"

"I hope I'll be the last."

She began to wring out the bottom of her skirt, and he was on his knees at once to do it for her.

"That will do very nicely," she presently said, the color billowing her cheeks.

He gathered wood and lit a fire, being fortunate enough to find his match-case had been waterproof. He piled on dry branches till the fire roared and licked out for the moisture in their clothes.

"I've been wondering how you happened to see me in the water," he said. "You were riding past, I expect?"

"No, I was sketching. I saw you when you came up to eat your lunch, and I watched you go back to the river."

"Do you live near here, then?" he asked.

"About three miles away."

"And you were watching me all the time?" He put his statement as a question.

"No, I wasn't," the young woman answered indignantly. "You happened to be in the landscape."

"A blot in it," he suggested. "A hop-toad splashing in the puddle."

The every-ready dimples flashed out at this. "You did make quite a splash when you went in. The fish must have thought it was a whale."

"And when I told you the water was fine, and you came in, too, they probably took you for a naiad."

She thanked him with an informal little nod.

"I thought you Anglo-Saxons did not give compliments."

"I don't," he immediately answered.

"Oh! If that isn't another one, I'm mistaken, sir." She turned indifferently away, apparently of the opinion that she had been quite friendly enough to this self-possessed young stranger.

Rewinding the lariat, she fastened it to the saddle, then swung to the seat before he could step forward to aid her.

"I hope you will suffer no bad effects from your bath," he said.

"I shall not; but I'm afraid you will. You were in long enough to get thoroughly chilled. *Adios, senor.*"

He called to her before the pony had taken a dozen steps:

"Your handkerchief, *senorita!*"

She turned in the saddle and waited for him to bring it. He did so, and she noticed that he limped badly.

"You have hurt yourself," she said quickly.

"I must have jammed my knee against a rock," he explained. "Nothing serious."

"But it pains?"

"Just enough to let me know it's there."

Frowning, she watched him.

"Is it a bruise or a sprain?"

"A wrench, I think. It will be all right if I favor it"

"Favor it? Except the ranch, there is no place nearer than seven miles. You are staying at Corbett's, I presume?"

"Yes."

"You can't walk back there to-night. That is certain." She slipped from the saddle. "You'll have to go back to the ranch with me, sir. I can walk very well."

He felt a wave of color sweep his face.

"I couldn't take the horse and let you walk."

"That is nonsense, sir. You can, and you shall."

"If I am to take your horse I need not saddle myself upon your hospitality. I can ride back to Corbett's, and send the horse home to-morrow."

"It is seven miles to Miguel's, and Corbett's is three beyond that. No doctor would advise that long ride before your knee receives attention, I think, sir, you will have to put up with the ranch till to-morrow."

"You ain't taking my intention right. All I meant was that I didn't like to unload myself on your folks; but if you say I'm to do it I'll be very happy to be your guest." He said it with a touch of boyish embarrassment she found becoming.

"We'll stop at the top of the hill and take on my drawing things," she told him.

He need have had no fears for her as a walker, for she was of the elect few born to grace of motion. Slight she was, yet strong; the delicacy that breathed from her was of the spirit, and consisted with perfect health. No Grecian nymph could have trod with lighter or surer step nor have unconsciously offered to the eye more supple and beautiful lines of limb and body.

Never had the young man seen before anybody whose charm

went so poignantly to the root of his emotions. Every turn of the head, the set of the chin, the droop of the long, thick lashes on the soft cheek, the fling of a gesture, the cadence of her voice; they all delighted and fascinated him. She was a living embodiment of joy-in-life, of love personified.

She packed her sketches and her paraphernalia with businesslike directness, careless of whether he did or did not see her water-colors. A movement of his hand stayed her as she took from, the easel the one upon which she had been engaged.

It represented the sun-drenched slope below them, with the little gulch dressed riotously in its gala best of yellows.

"You've got that fine," he told her enthusiastically.

She shook her head, unmoved by praise which did not approve itself to her judgment as merited.

"No, I didn't get it at all. A great artist might get the wonder of it; but I can't."

"It looks good to me," he said.

"Then I'm afraid you're not a judge," she smiled.

From where they stood a trail wound along the ridge and down into a valley beyond. At the farther edge of this, nestling close to the hills that took root there, lay the houses of a ranch.

"That is where I live," she told him.

He thought it a lovely spot, almost worthy of her, but obviously he could not tell her so. Instead, he voiced an alien thought that happened to intrude:

"Do you know Senorita Valdes? But of course you must."

She flung a quick glance at him, questioning.

"Yes, I know her."

"She lives somewhere round here, too, does she not?"

Her arm swept round in a comprehensive gesture. "Over that way, too."

"Do you know her well?"

An odd smile dimpled her face.

"Sometimes I think I do, and then again I wonder."

"I have been told she is beautiful."

"Beauty is in the beholder's eyes, *senor*. Valencia Valdes is as Heaven made her."

"I have no doubt; but Heaven took more pains with some of us than others—it appears."

Again the dark eyes under the long lashes swept him from the curly head to the lean, muscular hands, and approved silently the truth of his observation. The clean lithe build of the man, muscles packed so that they rippled smoothly like those of a panther, appealed to her trained eyes. So, too, did the quiet, steady eyes in the bronzed face, holding as they did the look of competent alertness that had come from years of frontier life.

"You are interested in Miss Valdes?" she asked politely.

"In a way of speaking, I am. She is one of the reasons why I came here."

"Indeed! She would no doubt be charmed to know of your interest," still with polite detachment.

"My interest ain't exactly personal; then again it is," he contributed.

"A sort of an impersonal personal interest?"

"Yes; though I don't quite know what that means."

"Then I can't be expected to," she laughed.

His laughter joined hers; but presently he recurred to his question:

"You haven't told me yet about Miss Valdes. Is she as lovely as they say she is?"

"I don't know just how lovely they say she is. Sometimes I have thought her very passable; then again—" She broke off with a defiant little laugh. "Don't you know, sir, that you mustn't ask one lady to praise the beauty of another?"

"I suppose I may ask questions?" he said, much amused.

"It depends a little on the questions."

"Is she tall?"

"Rather. About as tall as I am."

"And dark, of course, since she is a Spanish *senorita*"

"Yes, she is dark."

"Slim and graceful, I expect?"

"She is slender."

"I reckon she banks a heap on that blue blood of hers?"

"Yes; she is prouder of it than there is really any need of, though I think probably her pride is unconscious and a matter of habit."

"I haven't been able to make out yet whether you like her," he laughed.

"I don't see what my liking has to do with it."

"I expect to meet her, and I want to use your judgment to base mine on."

"Oh, you expect to meet her?"

She said it lightly, yet with a certain emphasis that he noted.

"Don't you think she will let me? Do I have to show blue blood before I can be presented? One of my ancestors came over on the *Mayflower*. Will that do?"

Her raillery met his.

"That ought to do, I should think. I suppose you have brought genealogical proofs with you?"

"I clean forgot. Won't you please get on and ride now? I feel like a false alarm, playing the invalid on you, ma'am."

"No; I'll walk. We're almost at the ranch. It's just under this hill. But there's one thing I want to ask of you as a favor."

"It's yours," he replied briefly.

She seemed to struggle with some emotion before she spoke:

"Please don't mention Valencia Valdes while you are at the ranch. I—I have reasons, sir."

"Certainly; I'll do as you prefer."

To himself he thought that there was probably a feud of some kind between the two families that might make a mention of the name unpleasant. "And that reminds me that I don't know what your name is. Mine is Muir—Richard Muir."

"And mine is Maria Yuste."

He offered her his brown hand. "I'm right happy to meet you, Senorita Maria."

"Welcome to the Yuste *hacienda, senor*. What is ours is yours, so long as you are our guest. I pray you make yourself at home," she said as they rode into the courtyard.

Two Mexican lads came running forward; and one whom she called Pedro took the horse, while the other went into the house to attend to a quick command she gave in Spanish.

The man who had named himself Richard Muir followed his hostess through a hall, across an open court, and into a living-room carpeted with Navajo rugs, at the end of which was a great open fireplace bearing a Spanish motto across it.

Large windows, set three feet deep in the thick adobe walls, were filled with flowers or padded with sofa pillows for seats. One of these his hostess indicated to the limping man.

"If you will be seated here for the present, sir, your room will be ready very soon."

A few minutes later the fisherman found himself in a large bedroom. He was seated in an easy-chair before a crackling fire of *pinon* knots.

A messenger had been dispatched for a doctor, Senorita Yuste had told him, and in the meantime he was to make himself quite at home.

CHAPTER IV

AT THE YUSTE HACIENDA

The wrench to the fisherman's knee proved more serious than he had anticipated. The doctor pronounced it out of the question that he should be moved for some days at least.

The victim was more than content, because he was very much interested in the young woman who had been his rescuer, and because it gave him a chance to observe at first hand the remains of the semifeudal system that had once obtained in New Mexico and California.

It was easy for him to see that Senorita Maria Yuste was still considered by her dependents as a superior being, one far removed from them by the divinity of caste that hedged her in. They gave her service; and she, on her part, looked out for their needs, and was the patron saint to whom they brought all their troubles.

It was an indolent, happy life the peons on the estate led, patriarchal in its nature, and far removed from the throb of the money-mad world. They had enough to eat and to wear. There was a roof over their heads. There were girls to be loved, dances to be danced, and guitars to be strummed. Wherefore, then, should the young men feel the spur of an ambition to take the world by the throat and wring success from it?

It had been more years than he could remember since this young American had taken a real holiday except for an occasional fishing trip on the Gunnison or into Wyoming. He had lived a life of activity. Now for the first time he learned how to be lazy. To dawdle indolently on one of the broad porches, while Miss Yuste sat beside him and busied herself over some needlework, was a sensuous delight that filled him with content. He felt that he would like to bask there in the warm sunshine forever. After all, why should he pursue wealth and success when love and laughter waited for him in this peaceful valley chosen of the gods?

The fourth morning of his arrival he hobbled out to the south porch after breakfast, to find his hostess in corduroy skirt, high laced boots, and pinched-in sombrero. She was drawing on a pair of driving gauntlets. One of the stable boys was standing beside a rig he had just driven to the house.

The young woman flung a flashing smile at her guest.

"Good day, Senor Muir. I hope you had a good night's rest, and that your knee did not greatly pain you?"

"I feel like a colt in the pasture—fit for anything. But the doctor won't have it that way. He says I'm an invalid," returned the young man whimsically.

"The doctor ought to know," she laughed.

"I expect it won't do me any harm to lie still for a day or two. We Americans all have the git-up-and-dust habit. We got to keep going, though Heaven knows what we're going for sometimes."

Though he did not know it, her interest in him was considerable, though certainly critical. He was a type outside of her experience, and, by the law of opposites, attracted her. Every line of him showed tremendous driving power, force, energy. He was not without some touch of Western swagger; but it went well with the air of youth to which his boyish laugh and wavy, sun-reddened hair contributed.

The men of her station that she knew were of one pattern, indolent, well-bred aristocrats, despisers of trade and of those who indulged in it more than was necessary to live. But her mother had been an American girl, and there was in her blood a strong impulse toward the great nation of which her father's people were not yet in spirit entirely a part.

"I have to drive to Antelope Springs this morning. It is not a rough trip at all. If you would care to see the country—"

She paused, a question in her face. Her guest jumped at the chance.

"There is nothing I should like better. If you are sure it will be no inconvenience."

"I am sure I should not have asked you if I had not wanted you," she said; and he took it as a reproof.

She drove a pair of grays that took the road with the spirit of racers. The young woman sat erect and handled the reins masterfully, the while Muir leaned back and admired the steadiness of the slim, strong wrists, the businesslike directness with which she gave herself to her work, the glow of life whipped into her eyes and cheeks by the exhilaration of the pace.

"I suppose you know all about these old land-grants that

were made when New Mexico was a Spanish colony and later when it was a part of Mexico," he suggested.

Her dark eyes rested gravely on him an instant before she answered: "Most of us that were brought up on them know something of the facts."

"You are familiar with the Valdes grant?"

"Yes."

"And with the Moreno grant, made by Governor Armijo?"

"Yes."

"The claims conflict, do they not?"

"The Moreno grant is taken right from the heart of the Valdes grant. It includes all the springs, the valleys, the irrigable land; takes in everything but the hilly pasture land in the mountains, which, in itself, is valueless."

"The land included in this grant is of great value?"

"It pastures at the present time fifty thousand sheep and about twelve thousand head of cattle."

"Owned by Miss Valdes?"

"Owned by her and her tenants."

"She's what you call a cattle queen, then. Literally, the cattle on a thousand hills are hers."

"As they were her father's and her grandfather's before her, to be held in trust for the benefit of about eight hundred tenants," she answered quietly.

"Tell me more about it. The original grantee was Don Bartolome de Valdes, was he not?"

"Yes. He was the great-great-grandson of Don Alvaro de Valdes y Castillo, who lost his head because he was a braver and a better man than the king. Don Bartolome, too, was a great soldier and ruler. He was generous and public-spirited to a fault; and when the people of this province suffered from Indian raids he distributed thousands of sheep to relieve their distress."

"Bully for the old boy. He was a real philanthropist."

"Not at all. He *had* to do it. His position required it of him."

"That was it, eh?"

Her dusky eyes questioned him.

"You couldn't understand, I suppose, since you are an American, how he was the father and friend of all the people in these parts; how his troopers and *vaqueros* were a defense to the whole province?"

"I think I can understand that."

"So it was, even to his death, that he looked out for the poor peons dependent upon him. His herds grew mighty; and he asked of Facundo Megares, governor of the royal province, a grant of land upon which to pasture them. These herds were for his people; but they were in his name and belonged to him. Why should he not have been given land for them, since his was the sword that had won the land against the Apaches?"

"You ain't heard me say he shouldn't have had it"

"So the *alcalde* executed the act of possession for a tract, to be bounded on the south by Crow Spring, following its cordillera to the Ojo del Chico, east to the Pedornal range, north to the Ojo del Cibolo—Buffalo Springs—and west to the great divide. It was a princely estate, greater than the State of Delaware; and Don Bartolome held it for the King of Spain, and ruled over it with powers of life and death, but always wisely and generously, like the great-hearted gentleman he was."

"Bully for him."

"And at his death his son ruled in his stead; and *his* only son died in the Spanish-American War, as a lieutenant of volunteers in the United States Army. He was shot before Santiago."

The voice died away in her tremulous throat; and he wondered if it could be possible that this girl had been betrothed to the young soldier. But presently she spoke again, cheerfully and lightly:

"Wherefore, it happens that there remains only a daughter of the house of Valdes to carry the burden that should have been her brother's, to look out for his people, and to protect them both against themselves and others. She may fail; but, if I know her, the failure will not be because she has not tried."

"Good for her. I'd like to shake her aristocratic little paw and tell her to buck in and win."

"She would no doubt be grateful for your sympathy," the young woman answered, flinging a queer little look of irony at him.

"But what's the hitch about the Valdes grant? Why is there a doubt of its legality?"

She smiled gaily at him.

"No person who desires to remain healthy has any doubts in this neighborhood. We are all partizans of Valencia Valdes; and many of her tenants are such warm followers that they would not think twice about shedding blood in defense of her title. You must remember that they hold through her right. If she were dispossessed so would they be."

"Is that a threat? I mean, would it be if I were a claimant?" he asked, meeting her smile pleasantly.

"Oh, no. Miss Valdes would regret any trouble, and so should I." A shadow crossed her face as she spoke. "But she could not prevent her friends from violence, I am afraid. You see, she is only a girl, after all. They would move without her knowledge. I know they would."

"How would they move? Would it be a knife in the dark?"

His gray eyes, which had been warm as summer sunshine on a hill, were now fixed on her with chill inscrutability.

"I don't know. It might be that. Very likely." He saw the pulse in her throat beating fast as she hesitated before she plunged on. "A warning is not a threat. If you know this Senor Gordon, tell him to sell whatever claim he has. Tell him, at least, to fight from a distance; not to come to this valley himself. Else his life would be at hazard."

"If he is a man that will not keep him away. He will fight for what is his all the more because there is danger. What's more, he'll do his fighting on the ground—unless he's a quitter."

She sighed.

"I was afraid so."

"But you have not told me yet the alleged defect in the Valdes claim. There must be some point of law upon which the thing hangs."

"It is claimed that Don Bartolome did not take up his actual residence on the grant, as the law required. Then, too, he himself was later governor of the province, and while he was president of the Ayuntamiento at Tome he officially indorsed some small grants of land made from this estate. He did this because he wanted the country developed, and was willing to give part of what he had to his neighbors; but I suppose the contestant will claim this showed he had abandoned his grant."

"I see. Title not perfected," he summed up briefly.

"We deny it, of course—I mean, Miss Valdes does. She shows that in his will the old *don* mentions it, and that her father lived there without interruption, even though Manuel Armijo later granted the best of it to Jose Moreno."

"It would be pretty tough for her to be fired out now. I reckon she's attached to the place, her and her folks having lived there so long," the young man mused aloud.

"Her whole life is wrapped up in it. It is the home of her people. She belongs to it, and it to her," the girl answered.

"Mebbe this Gordon is a white man. I reckon he wouldn't drive her out. Like as not he'd fix up a compromise. There's enough for both."

She shook her head decisively.

"No. It would have to be a money settlement. Miss Valdes's people are settled all over the estate. Some of them have bought small ranches. You see, she couldn't—throw them down—as you Americans say."

"That's right," he agreed. "Well, I shouldn't wonder but it can be fixed up some way."

They had been driving across a flat cactus country, and for some time had been approaching the grove of willows into which she now turned. Some wooden barns, a corral, an adobe house, and outhouses marked the place as one of the more ambitious ranches of the valley.

An old Mexican came forward with a face wreathed in smiles.

"Buenos, Dona Maria," he cried, in greeting.

"*Buenos,* Antonio. This gentleman is Mr. Richard Muir."

"*Buenos, senor.* A friend of Dona Maria is a friend of Antonio."

"The older people call me '*dona,*'" the girl explained. "I suppose they think it strange a girl should have to do with affairs, and so they think of me as '*dona,*' instead of '*senorita,*' to satisfy themselves."

A vague suspicion, that had been born in the young man's

mind immediately after his rescue from the river now recurred.

His first thought then had been that this young woman must be Valencia Valdes; but he had dismissed it when he had seen the initial M on her kerchief, and when she had subsequently left him to infer that such was not the case.

He remembered now in what respect she was held in the home *hacienda*; how everybody they had met had greeted her with almost reverence. It was not likely that two young heiresses, both of them beautiful orphans, should be living within a few miles of each other.

Besides, he remembered that this very Antelope Springs was mentioned in the deed of conveyance which he had lately examined before leaving the mining camp. She was giving orders about irrigating ditches as if she were owner.

It followed then that she must be Valencia Valdes. There could be no doubt of it.

He watched her as she talked to old Antonio and gave the necessary directions. How radiant and happy she was in this life which had fallen to her; by inheritance! He vowed she should not be disinherited through any action of his. He owed her his life. At least, he could spare her this blow.

They drove home more silently than they had come. He was thinking over the best way to do what he was going to do. The evening before they had sat together in front of the fire in the living-room, while her old duenna had nodded in a big arm-chair. So they would sit to-night and to-morrow night.

He would send at once for the papers upon which his claim depended, and he would burn them before her eyes. After that they would be friends—and, in the end, much more than friends.

He was still dreaming his air-castle, when they drove through the gate that led to her home. In front of the porch a saddled bronco trailed its rein, and near by stood a young man in riding-breeches and spurs. He turned at the sound of wheels; and the man in the buggy saw that it was Manuel Pesquiera.

The Spaniard started when he recognized the other, and his eyes grew bright. He moved forward to assist the young woman in alighting; but, in spite of his bad knee, the Coloradoan was out of the rig and before him.

"*Buenos, amigo*" she nodded to Don Manuel, lightly releasing the hand of Muir.

"*Buenos, senorita*" returned that young man. "I behold you are already acquaint' with Mr. Richard Gordon, whose arrival is to me very unexpect'."

She seemed to grow tall before her guest's eyes; to stand in a kind of proud splendor that had eclipsed her girlish slimness. The dark eyes under the thick lashes looked long and searchingly at him.

"Mr. Richard Gordon? I understand this gentleman's name to be Muir," she made voice gently.

Dick laughed with a touch of shame. Now once in his life he wished he could prove an alibi. For, under the calm judgment of that steady gaze, the thing he had done seemed scarce defensible.

"Don Manuel has it right, *senorita*. Gordon is my name;

Muir, too, for that matter. Richard Muir Gordon is what I was christened."

The underlying red of her cheeks had fled and left them clear olive. One might have thought the scornful eyes had absorbed all the fire of her face.

"So you have lied to me, sir?"

"Let me lay the facts before you, first. That's a hard word, *senorita*."

"You gave your name to me as Muir, You imposed yourself on my hospitality under false pretenses. You are only a spy, come to my house to mole for evidence against me."

"No—no!" he cried sharply. "You will remember that I did not want to come. I foresaw that it might be awkward, but I did not foresee this."

"That you would be found out before you had won your end? I believe you, sir," she retorted contemptuously.

"I see I'm condemned before I'm heard."

"Will any explanation alter the facts? Are you not a liar and a cheat? You gave me a false name to spy out the land."

"Am I the only one that gave a wrong name?" he asked.

"That is different," she flamed. "You had made a mistake and, half in sport, I encouraged you in it. But you seem to have found out my real name since. Yet you still accepted what I had to offer, under a false name, under false pretenses. You questioned me about the grants. You have lived a lie from first to last."

"It ain't as bad as you say, ma'am. Don Manuel had told me it wasn't safe to come here in my own name. I didn't care about the safety, but I wanted to see the situation exactly as it was. I didn't know who you were when I came here. I took you to be Miss Maria Yuste. I—"

"My name is Maria Yuste Valencia Valdes," the young woman explained proudly. "When, may I ask, did you discover who I was?"

"I guessed it at Antelope Springs."

"Then why did you not tell me then who you are? Surely that was the time to tell me. My deception did you no harm; yours was one no man of honor could have endured after he knew who I was."

"I didn't aim to keep it up very long. I meant, in a day or two—"

"A day or two," she cried, in a blaze of scorn. "After you had found out all I had to tell; after you had got evidence to back your robber-claim; after you had made me breathe the same air so long with a spy?"

Her face was very white; but she faced him in her erect slimness, with her dark eyes fixed steadily on him.

"You ain't quite fair to me; but let that pass for the present. When I asked you about the grants didn't you guess who I was? Play square with me. Didn't you have a notion?"

A flood of spreading color swept back into her face.

"No, I didn't. I thought perhaps you were an agent of the claimant; but I didn't know you were passing under a false name, that you were aware in whose house you were staying. I thought you an honest man, on the wrong side—nothing so contemptible as a spy."

"That idea's fixed in your mind, is it?" he asked quietly.

"Beyond any power of yours to remove it," she flashed back.

"The facts, Senor Gordon, speak loud," put in Pesquiera derisively.

Dick Gordon paid not the least attention to him. His gaze was fastened on the girl whose contempt was lashing him.

"Very well, Miss Valdes. Well let it go at that just now. All I've got to say is that some day you'll hate yourself for what you have just said."

Neither of them had raised their voices from first to last. Hers had been low and intense, pulsing with the passion that would out. His had held its even way.

"I hate myself now, that I have had you here so long, that I have been the dupe of a common cheat."

"All right. 'Nough said, ma'am. More would certainly be surplusage. I'll not trouble you any longer now. But I want you to remember that there's a day coming when you'll travel a long way to take back all of what you've just been saying. I want to thank you for all your kindness to me. I'm always at your service for what you did for me. Good-bye, Miss Valdes, for the present."

"I am of impression, sir, that you go not too soon," said Pesquiera suavely.

Miss Valdes turned on her heel and swept up the steps of the porch; but she stopped an instant before she entered the house to say over her shoulder:

"A buggy will be at your disposal to take you to Corbett's. If it is convenient, I should like to have you go to-night."

He smiled ironically.

"I'll not trouble you for the buggy, *senorita*. If I'm all you say I am, likely I'm a horse thief, too. Anyhow, we won't risk it. Walking's good enough for me."

"Just as you please," she choked, and forthwith disappeared into the house.

Gordon turned from gazing after her to find the little Spaniard bowing before him.

"Consider me at your service, Mr. Gordon—"

"Can't use you," cut in Dick curtly.

"I was remarking that, as her kinsman, I, Don Manuel Pesquiera, stand prepared to make good her words. What the Senorita Valdes says, I say, too."

"Then don't say it aloud, you little monkey, or I'll throw you over the house," Dick promised immediately.

Don Manuel clicked his heels together and twirled his black mustache.

"I offer you, sir, the remedy of a gentleman. You, sir, shall choose the weapons."

The Anglo-Saxon laughed in his face.

"Good. Let it be toasting-forks, at twenty paces."

The challenger drew himself up to his full five feet six.

"You choose to be what you call droll. Sir, I give you the word, poltroon—*lache*—coward."

"Oh, go chase yourself."

One of Pesquiera's little gloved hands struck the other's face with a resounding slap. Next instant he was lifted from his feet and tucked under Dick's arm.

There he remained, kicking and struggling, in a manner most undignified for a blue blood of Castile, while the Coloradoan stepped leisurely forward to the irrigating ditch which supplied water for the garden and the field of grain behind. This was now about two feet deep, and running strong. In it was deposited, at full length, the clapper little person of Don Manuel Pesquiera, after which Dick Gordon turned and went limping down the road.

From the shutters of her room a girl had looked down and seen it all. She saw Don Manuel rescue himself from the ditch, all dripping with water. She saw him gesticulating wildly, as he cursed the retreating foe, before betaking himself hurriedly from view to the rear of the house, probably to dry himself and nurse his rage the while. She saw Gordon go on his limping way without a single backward glance.

Then she flung herself on her bed and burst into tears.

CHAPTER V

"AN OPTIMISTIC GUY"

Dick Gordon hobbled up the road, quite unaware for some time that he had a ricked knee. His thoughts were busy with the finale that had just been enacted. He could not keep from laughing ruefully at the difference between it and the one of his day-dreams. He was too much of a Westerner not to see the humor of the comedy in which he had been forced to take a leading part, but he had insight enough to divine that it was much more likely to prove melodrama than farce.

Don Manuel was not the man to sit down under such an insult as he had endured, even though he had brought it upon himself. It would too surely be noised round that the *Americano* was the claimant to the estate, in which event he was very likely to play the part of a sheath for restless stilettos.

This did not trouble him as much as it would have done some men. The real sting of the episode lay in Valencia Valdes' attitude toward him. He had been kicked out for his unworthiness. He had been cast aside as a spy and a sneak.

The worst of it was that he felt his clumsiness deserved no less an issue to the adventure. Confound that little Don

Manuel for bobbing up at such an inconvenient time! It was fierce luck.

He stopped his tramp up the hill, and looked back over the valley. Legally it was all his. So his Denver lawyers had told him, after looking the case over carefully. The courts would decide for him in all probability; morally he had not the shadow of a claim. The valley in justice belonged to those who had settled in it and were using it for their needs. His claim was merely a paper one. It had not a scintilla of natural justice back of it.

He resumed his journey. By this time his knee was sending telegrams of pain to headquarters. He cut an aspen by the roadside and trimmed it to a walking-stick and, as he went forward, leaned more and more heavily upon it.

"I'm going to have a game leg for fair if I don't look out," he told himself ruefully. "This right pin surely ain't good for a twelve-mile tramp."

It was during one of his frequent stops to rest that a buggy appeared round the turn from the same direction he had come. It drew to a halt in front of him, and the lad who was driving got out.

"Senorita Maria sends a carriage for Senor Gordon to take him to Corbett's," he said.

Dick was on hand with a sardonic smile.

"Tell the *senorita* that Mr. Gordon regrets having put her to so much trouble, but that he needs the exercise and prefers to walk."

"The *senorita* said I was to insist, *senor*."

"Tell your mistress that I'm very much obliged to her, but have made other arrangements. Explain to her I appreciate the offer just the same."

The lad hesitated, and Dick pushed him into decision.

"That's all right, Juan—Jose—Pedro—Francisco—whatever your name is. You've done your levelest. Now, hike back to the ranch. *Vamos! Sabe.*"

"*Si, senor.*"

Dick heard the wheels disappear in the distance, and laughed aloud.

"That young woman's conscience is hurting her. I reckon this tramp to Corbett's is going to worry her tender heart about as much as it does me, and I've got to sweat blood before I get through with it. Here goes again, Dicky."

Every step sent a pain shooting through him, but he was the last man to give up on that account what he had undertaken.

"She let me go without any lunch," he chuckled. "I'll bet that troubles her some, too, when she remembers. She's got me out of the house, but I'll bet the last strike in the Nancy K. against a dollar Mex that she ain't got me out of her mind by a heap."

A buggy appeared in sight driven by a stout, red-faced old man. Evidently he was on his way to the ranch.

"Who, hello, Doctor! I'm plumb glad to see you; couldn't wait till you came, and had just to start out to meet you," cried Dick.

He stood laughing at the amazement in the face of the doctor, who was in two minds whether to get angry or not.

"Doggone your hide, what are you doing here? Didn't I tell you not to walk more than a few steps?" that gentleman protested.

"But you didn't leave me a motor-car and, my visit being at an end, I ce'tainly had to get back to Corbett's." As he spoke he climbed slowly into the rig. "That leg of mine is acting like sixty, Doctor. When you happened along I was wondering how in time I was ever going to make it."

"You may have lamed yourself for life. It's the most idiotic thing I ever heard of. I don't see why Miss Valdes let you come. Dad blame it, have I got to watch my patients like a hen does its chicks? Ain't any of you got a lick of sense? Why didn't she send a rig if you had to come?" the doctor demanded.

"Seems to me she did mention a rig, but I thought I'd rather walk," explained Gordon casually, much amused at Dr. Watson's chagrined wonder.

"Walk!" snorted the physician. "You'll not walk, but be carried into an operating-room if you're not precious lucky. You deserve to lose that leg, and I don't say you won't."

"I'm an optimistic guy, Doctor. I'll say it for you. I ain't got any legs to spare."

"Huh! Some people haven't got the sense of a chicken with its head cut off."

"Now you're shouting. Go for me, Doc. Then, mebbe, I'll do better next time."

The doctor gave up this incorrigible patient and relapsed into silence, from which he came occasionally with an explosive "Huh!" Once he broke out with: "Didn't she feed you well enough, or was it just that you didn't *know* when you were well off?"

For he was aware that his patient's fever was rising and, like a good practitioner, he fumed at such useless relapse.

The knee had been doing fine. Now there would be the devil to pay with it. The utter senselessness of the proceeding irritated Watson. What in Mexico had got into the young idiot to make him do such a fool thing? The doctor guessed at a quarrel between him and Miss Valdes. But the close-mouthed American gave him no grounds upon which to base his suspicion.

The first thing that Dick did after reaching Corbett's was to send two telegrams. One was addressed to Messrs. Hughes & Willets, 411-417 Equitable Building, Denver, Colorado; the other went to Stephen Davis, Cripple Creek, of the same state.

Doctor Watson hustled his patient to bed and did his best to relieve the increasing pain in the swollen knee. He swore gently and sputtered and fumed as he worked, restraining himself only when Mrs. Corbett came into the room with hot water, towels, compresses, and other supplies.

"What about a nurse?" Watson wanted to know of Mrs. Corbett, a large motherly woman whose kind heart always found room in it for the weak and helpless.

"I got no room for one. Juanita and I will take care of him. The work's slack now. We'll have time."

"He's going to take a heap of nursing," the doctor answered, rubbing his unshaven chin dubiously with the palm of his hand. "See how the fever's climbed up even in the last half hour. That boy's going to be a mighty sick *hombre*."

"I'm used to nursing, and Juanita is the best help I ever had, if she *is* a Mexican. You may trust him to us."

"Hmp! I wasn't thinking of him, but of you. Couldn't be in better hands, but it's an imposition for him to go racing all over these hills with a game leg and expect you to pull him through."

Before midnight Dick was in a raging fever. In delirium he tossed from side to side, sometimes silent for long stretches, then babbling fragments of forgotten scenes rescued by his memory automatically from the wild and picturesque past of the man. Now he fancied himself again a schoolboy, now a ranger in Arizona, now mushing on the snow trails of Alaska. At times he would imagine that he was defending his mine against attacking strikers, or that he was combing the Rincons for horse thieves. Out of his turbid past flared for an instant dramatic moments of comedy or tragedy. These passed like the scenes of a motion-picture story, giving place to something else.

In the end he came back always to the adventure he was still living.

"You're a spy.... You're a liar and a cheat.... You imposed yourself upon my hospitality under false pretenses.... I hate myself for breathing the same air as you." He would break off to laugh foolishly, in a high-pitched note of derision at himself. "Stand up, Dick Gordon, and hear the lady tell you what a coyote you are. Stan' up and face the music, you quitter. Liar... spy... cheat! That's you, Dick Gordon, un'erstand?"

Or the sick mind of the man would forget for the moment that they had quarreled. His tongue would run over conversations that they had had, cherishing and repeating over and over again her gay little quips and sallies or her light phrases.

"Valencia Valdes is as God made her. Now you're throwing sixes, ma'am. Sure she's like that. The devil helped a heap to make most of us what we are, but I reckon God made that little lady early in the mo'ning when He was feeling fine.... Say, I wish you'd look at me like that again and light up with another of them dimply smiles. I got a surprise for you, Princess of the Rio Chama. Honest, I have. Sure as you're a foot high.... Never you mind what it is. Just you wait a while and I'll spring it when the time's good and ready. I got to wait till the papers come. See?... Oh, shucks, you're sore at me again! Liar... cheat... spy! Say, I know when I've had a-plenty. She don't like me. I'm goin' to pull my freight for the Kotzebue country up in Alaska.

'On the road to Kotzebue, optimistic through and through,
We'll hit the trail together, boy, once more, jest me an'
you.'

Funny how women act, ain't it? Stand up and take your medicine—liar... cheat ... spy! She said it, didn't she? Well, then, it must be so. What you kickin' about?"

So he would run on until the fever had for the hour exhausted itself and he lay still among the pillows. Sometimes he talked the strong language of the man in battle with other men, but even in his oaths there was nothing of vulgarity.

Mrs. Corbett took the bulk of the nursing on her own broad fat shoulders, but during the day she was often relieved by her maid while she got a few hours of sleep.

Juanita was a slim, straight girl not yet nineteen. Even before his sickness Dick, with the instinct for deference to all women of self-respect that obtains among frontiersmen, had won the gratitude of the shy creature. There was something wild and sylvan about her sweet grace. The deep, soft eyes in the brown oval face were as appealing as those of a doe wounded by the hunter.

She developed into a famous nurse. Low-voiced and soft-footed, she would coax the delirious man to lie down when he grew excited or to take his medicine according to the orders of the doctor.

It was on the third day after Gordon's return to Corbett's that Juanita heard a whistle while she was washing dishes after supper in the kitchen. Presently she slipped out of the back door and took the trail to the corral. A man moved forward out of the gloom to meet her.

"Is it you, Pablo?"

A slender youth, lean-flanked and broad-shouldered, her visitor turned out to be. His outstretched hands went forward swiftly to meet hers.

"Juanita, light of my life?" he cried softly. "*Corazon mia!*"

She submitted with a little reluctant protest to his caress. "I have but a minute, Pablo. The *senora* wants to walk over to Dolan's place. I am to stay with the sick American."

He exploded with low, fierce energy. "A thousand curses take the gringo! Why should you nurse him? Is he not an enemy to the *senorita*—to all in the valley who have bought from her or her father or her grandfather? Is he not here to throw us out—a thief, a spy, a snake in the grass?"

"No, he is not. *Senor* Gordon is good... and kind."

"Bah! You are but a girl. He gives you soft words—and so—
" The jealousy in him flared suddenly out. He caught his
sweetheart tightly by the arm. "Has he made love to you, this
gringo? Has he whispered soft, false lies in your ear, Juanita?
If he has—"

She tried to twist free from him. "You are hurting my arm,
Pablo," the girl cried.

"It is my heart you hurt, *nina*. Is it true that this thief has
stolen the love of my Juanita?"

"You are a fool, Pablo. He has never said a hundred words to
me. All through his sickness he has talked and talked—but it
is of *Senorita* Valdes that he has raved."

"So. He will rob her of all she has and yet can talk of loving
her. Do you not see he is a villain, that he has the forked
tongue, as old Bear Paw, the Navajo, says of all gringoes?
But let Senor Gordon beware. His time is short. He will not
live to drive us from the valley. So say I. So say all the men
in the valley."

"No—no! I will not have it, Pablo. You do not know. This
Senor Gordon is good. He would not drive us away." Her
arms slid around the neck of her lover and she pleaded with
him impetuously. "You must not let them hurt him, for it is a
kind heart he has."

"Why should I interfere? He is only a gringo. Let him die. I
tell you he means harm to all of us."

"I do not know my Pablo when he talks like this. My Pablo
was always kind and good and of a soft heart. I do not love

him when he is cruel."

"It is then that you love the American," he cried. "Did I not know it? Did I not say so?"

"You say much that is foolish, *muchacho*. The American is a stranger to me... and you are Pablo. But how can I love you when your heart is full of cruelty and jealousy and revenge? Go to the Blessed Virgin and confess before the good priest your sins, *amigo*."

"*Amigo!* Since when have I been friend to you and not lover, Juanita? I know well for how long—since this gringo with the white face crossed your trail."

Suddenly she flung away from him. "*Muy bien!* You shall think as you please. Adios, my friend with the head of a donkey! *Adios, icabron!*"

She was gone, light as the wind, flying with swift feet down the trail to the house. Sulkily he waited for her to come out again, but the girl did not appear. He gave her a full half hour before he swung to the saddle and turned the head of his pony toward the Valdes' hacienda. A new and poignant bitterness surged in his heart. Had this stranger, who was bringing trouble to the whole valley, come between him and little Juanita, whom he had loved since they had been children? Had he stolen her heart with his devilish wiles? The hard glitter in the black eyes of the Mexican told that he would punish him if this were true.

His younger brother Pedro took the horse from him as he rode into the ranch plaza an hour later.

"You are to go to the *senorita* at once and tell her how the gringo is, Pablo." After a moment he added sullenly:

"*Maldito*, how is the son of a thief?"

"Sick, Pedro, sick unto death. The devil, as you say, may take him yet without any aid from us," answered Pablo Menendez brusquely.

"Why does the *senorita* send you every day to find out how he is? Can she not telephone? And why should she care what becomes of the traitor?" demanded Pedro angrily.

His brother shrugged. "How should I know?" He had troubles enough with the fancies of another woman without bothering about those of the *senorita*.

Valencia Valdes was on the porch waiting for her messenger.

"How is he, Pablo? Did you see the doctor and talk with him? What does he say?"

"*Si, senorita*. I saw Doctor Watson and he send you this letter. They say the American is a sick man—oh, very, very sick!"

The young woman dismissed him with a nod and hurried to her room. She read the letter from the doctor and looked out of one of the deep adobe windows into the starry night. It happened to be the same window from which she had last seen him go hobbling down the road. She rose and put out the light so that she could weep the more freely. It was hard for her to say why her heart was so heavy. To herself she denied that she cared for this jaunty debonair scoundrel. He was no doubt all she had told him on that day when she had driven him away.

Yes, but she had sent him to pain and illness... perhaps to death. The tears fell fast upon the white cheeks. Surely it was not her fault that he had been so obstinate. Yet—down in the depth of her heart she knew she loved the courage that had carried him with such sardonic derision out upon the road for the long tramp that had so injured him. And there was an inner citadel within her that refused to believe him the sneaking pup she had accused him of being. No man with such honest eyes, who stood so erect and graceful in the image of God, could be so contemptible a cur. There was something fine about the spirit of the man. She had sensed the kinship of it without being able to put a finger exactly upon the quality she meant. He might be a sinner, but it was hard to believe him a small and mean one. The dynamic spark of self-respect burned too brightly in his soul for that.

CHAPTER VI

JUANITA

The fifth day marked the crisis of Gordon's illness. After that he began slowly to mend.

One morning he awoke to a realization that he had been very ill. His body was still weak, but his mind was coherent again. A slender young woman moved about the room setting things in order.

"Aren't you Juanita?" he asked.

Her heart gave a leap. This was the first time he had recognized her. Sometimes in his delirium he had caught at her hand ind tried to kiss it, but always under the impression that she was Miss Valdes.

"*Si, senor*," she answered quietly.

"I thought so." He added after a moment, with the childlike innocence a sick person has upon first coming back to sanity: "There couldn't be two girls as pretty as you in this end of the valley, could there?"

Under her soft brown skin the color flooded Juanita's face.

"I—I don't know." She spoke in a flame of embarrassment, so abrupt had been his compliment and so sincere.

"I've been very sick, haven't I?"

She nodded. "Oh, *senor*, we have been—what you call—worried."

"Good of you, Juanita. Who has been taking care of me?"

"Mrs. Corbett."

"And Juanita?"

"Sometimes."

"Ah! That's good of you, too, *amiga*."

She recalled a phrase she had often heard an American rancher's daughter say. "I loved to do it, *senor*."

"But why? I'm your enemy, you know. You ought to hate me. Do you?"

Once again the swift color poured into the dark cheeks, even to the round birdlike throat.

"No, *senor*."

He considered this an instant before he accused her whimsically. "Then you're not a good girl. You should hate the devil, and I'm his agent. Any of your friends will tell you that."

"*Senor* Gordon is a joke."

He laughed weakly. "Am I? I'll bet I am, the fool way I acted."

"I mean a—what you call—a joker," she corrected.

"But ain't I your enemy, my little good Samaritan? Isn't that what all your people are saying?"

"I not care what they say."

"If I'm not your enemy, what am I?"

She made a great pretense of filling the ewer with water and gathering up the soiled towels.

"How about that, *nina*?" he persisted, turning toward her on the pillow with his unshaven face in his hand, a gentle quizzical smile in his eyes.

"I'm your... servant, *senor*," she flamed, after the embarrassment of silence had grown too great.

"No, no! Nothing like that. What do you say? Will you take me for a friend, even though I'm an enemy to the whole valley?"

Her soft, dark eyes flashed to meet his, timidly and yet with an effect of fine spirit.

"*Si, senor.*"

"Good. Shake hands on it, little partner."

She came forward reluctantly, as if she were pushed toward him by some inner compulsion. Her shy embarrassment, together with the sweetness of the glad emotion that trembled in her filmy eyes, lent her a rare charm.

For just an instant her brown fingers touched his, then she turned and fled from the room.

Mrs. Corbett presently bustled in, fat, fifty, and friendly.

"I can't hardly look you in the face," he apologized, with his most winning smile. "I reckon I've been a nuisance a-plenty, getting sick on your hands like a kid."

Mrs. Corbett answered his smile as she arranged the coverlets.

"You'll just have to be good for a spell to make up for it. No more ten-mile walks, Mr. Muir, till the knee is all right."

"I reckon you better call me Gordon, ma'am." His mind passed to what she had said about his walk. "Ce'tainly that was a fool *pasear* for a man to take. Comes of being pig-headed, Mrs. Corbett. And Doc Watson had told me not to use that game leg much. But, of course, I knew best," he sighed ruefully.

"Well, you've had your lesson. And you've worried all of us. Miss Valdes has called up two or three times a day on the phone and sent a messenger over every evening to find out how you were."

Dick felt the blood flush his face. "She has?" Then, after a little: "That's very kind of Miss Valdes."

"Yes. Everybody has been kind. Mr. Pesquiera has called up every day to inquire about you. He has been very anxious for you to recover."

A faint sardonic smile touched the white lips. "A fellow never knows how many friends he has till he needs them. So Don Manuel is in a hurry to have me get on my feet. That's surely right kind of him."

He thought he could guess why that proud and passionate son of Spain fretted to see him ill. The humiliation to which he had been subjected was rankling in his heart and would oppress him till he could wipe it out in action.

"You've got other friends, too, that have worried a lot," said Mrs. Corbett, as she took up some knitting.

"More friends yet? Say, ain't I rich? I didn't know how blamed popular I was till now," returned the invalid, with derisive irony. "Who is it this time I've got to be grateful for?"

"Mr. Davis."

"Steve Davis—from Cripple Creek, Colorado, God's Country?"

"Yes."

"Been writing about me, has he?"

Mrs. Corbett smiled. She had something up her sleeve. "First writing, then wiring."

"He's a kind of second dad to me. Expect the old rooster got anxious."

"Looks that way. Anyhow, he reached here last night."

Gordon got up on an elbow in his excitement. "Here? Here

now? Old Steve?"

She nodded her head and looked over her shoulder toward the dining-room. "In there eating his breakfast. He'll be through pretty soon. You see, he doesn't know you're awake."

Presently Davis came into the room. He walked to the bed and took both of his friend's hands in his. Tears were shining in his eyes.

"You darned old son-of-a-gun, what do you mean by scaring us like this? I've lost two years' growth on account of your foolishness, boy."

"Did Mrs. Corbett send for you?"

"No, I sent for myself soon as I found out how sick you was. Now hustle up and get well."

"I'm going to do just that"

Dick kept his word. Within a few days he was promoted to a rocking-chair on the porch. Here Juanita served his meals and waited on his demands with the shy devotion that characterized a change in her attitude to him. She laughed less than she did. His jokes, his claim upon her as his "little partner," his friendly gratitude, all served to embarrass her, and at the same time to fill her with a new and wonderful delight.

A week ago, when he had been lying before her asleep one day, she had run her little finger through one of his tawny curls and admired its crisp thickness. To her maiden fancy something of his strong virility had escaped even to this wayward little lock of hair. She had wondered then how the

Senorita Valdes could keep from loving this splendid fellow if he cared for her. All the more she wondered now, for her truant heart was going out to him with the swift ardent passion of her race. It was as a sort of god she looked upon him, as a hero of romance far above her humble hopes. She found herself longing for chances to wait upon him, to do little services that would draw the approving smile to his eyes.

Gordon was still in the porch-dwelling stage of convalescence when a Mexican rider swung from his saddle one afternoon with a letter from Manuel Pesquiera. The note was a formal one, written in the third person, and it wasted no words.

After reading it Dick tossed the sheet of engraved stationery across to his companion.

"Nothing like having good, anxious friends in a hurry to have you well, Steve," he said, with a smile.

The old miner read the communication. "Well, what's the matter with his hoping you'll be all right soon?"

"No reason why he shouldn't. It only shows what a Christian, forgiving disposition he's got. You see, that day I most walked my leg off I soused Mr. Pesquiera in a ditch."

"You—what?"

"Just what I say. I picked him up and dropped the gentleman in the nearest ditch. That's why he's so anxious to get me well."

"But—why for, boy?"

Dick laughed. "Can't you see, you old moss-back? He wants me well enough to call out for a duel."

"A duel." Davis stared at him dubiously. He did not know whether or not his friend was making game of him.

"Yes, sir. Pistols and coffee for two, waiter. That sort of thing."

"But folks don't fight duels nowadays," remonstrated the puzzled miner. "Anyhow, what's he want to fight about? I reckon you didn't duck him for nothing, did you? What was it all about?"

Dick told his tale of adventures, omitting only certain emotions that were his private property. He concluded with an account of the irrigating-ditch episode. "It ain't the custom in this part of the country to duck the blue bloods. Shouldn't wonder but what he's some hot under the collar. Writes like he sees red, don't you think, but aims to be polite and keep his shirt on."

Davis refused to treat the matter as a joke.

"I told you to let your lawyers 'tend to this, Dick, and for you not to poke your nose into this neck of the woods. But you had to come, and right hot off the reel you hand one to this Pesky fellow, or whatever you call him. Didn't I tell you that you can't bat these greasers over the head the way you can the Poles in the mines?"

"Sure you told me. You're always loaded with good advice, Steve. But what do you expect me to do when a fellow slaps my face?"

"They won't stand fooling with, these greasers. This Pesky

fellow is playing squarer than most would if he gives you warning to be ready with your six-gun. You take my advice, and you'll burn the wind out of this country. If you git this fellow, the whole pack of them will be on top of you, and don't you forget it, son."

"So you advise me to cut and run, do you?" said Dick.

"You bet."

"That's what you'd do, is it?"

"Sure thing. You can't clean out the whole of New Mexico."

"Quit your lying, Steve, you old war-horse. You'd see it out, just like I'm going to."

Davis scratched his grizzled poll and grinned, but continued to dispense good advice.

"You ain't aiming to mix with this whole blamed country, are you?"

The man in the chair sat up, his lean jaw set and his eyes gleaming.

"I've been called the scum o' the earth. I've been kicked out of her house as a fellow not decent enough to mix with honest folks. Only yesterday I got a letter from some of her people warning me to leave the country while I was still alive. This Pesquiera is camping on my trail."

"Maybe he ain't. You've only guessed that."

"Guess nothing. It's a cinch."

"What you going to do about it?"

"Nothing."

"But if he lays for you."

"Good enough. Let him go to it. I'm going through with this thing. I'm going to show them who's the best man. And when I've beat them to a standstill I've got a revenge ready that will make Miss Valdes eat humble pie proper. Yes, sir. I'm tied to this country till this thing's settled."

"Then there ain't any use saying any more about it. You always was a willful son-of-a-gun," testified his partner, with a grin. "And I reckon I'll have to stay with you to pack you home after the greasers have shot you up."

"Don't you ever think it, Steve," came back the cheerful retort. "I've got a hunch this is my lucky game. I'm sitting in to win, old hoss."

"What's your first play, Dick?"

"I made it last week, within twenty minutes of the time I got back here. Wired my lawyers to bring suit at once, and to push it for all it was worth."

"You can't settle it by the courts inside of a year, or mebbe two."

"I ain't aiming to settle it by the courts. All I want is they should know I've got them beat to a fare-ye-well in the courts. Their lawyers will let them know that mighty early, just as soon as they look the facts up. There ain't any manner of doubt about my legal claim. I guess Miss Valdes knows that already, but I want her to know it good and sure. Then

I'll paddle my own canoe. The law's only a bluff to make my hand better. I'm calling for that extra card for the looks of it, but my hand is full up without it"

"What's in your hand, anyhow, outside of your legal right? Looks to me they hold them all from ace down."

Dick laughed.

"You wait and see," he said.

CHAPTER VII

TWO MESSAGES

Because Dick had always lived a clean, outdoor life he rallied magnificently from the relapse into which his indiscretion had thrown him. For a few days Dr. Watson was worried by reason of the danger of blood-poisoning, but the splendid vitality of his patient quickly swept him out of danger. Soon he was hobbling round with a cane, and shortly after was able to take long rides over the country with his friend.

On one of these occasions, while they were climbing a hill trail, Davis broke a long silence to say aloud to himself: "There's just one way to account for it."

"Then it can't be a woman you're thinking of," Dick laughed; "for as far as I can make out there's always several ways to account for them, and the one you guess usually ain't right."

"You've said it, son. It's a woman. I been doing some inquiring about this Miss Valdes, and from all telling she's the prettiest ever."

"I could have told you that. It ain't a secret."

"I notice you didn't tell me."

"You didn't ask, you old geezer."

"Sho! You ain't such a clam when it comes to pretty girls. You didn't talk about her, because your haid's been full of her. It don't take a mind-reader to know that."

"You're ce'tainly a wizard, Steve," came back his partner dryly.

"I know you and your little ways by this time."

"So I'm in love, am I?"

"You're there, or traveling there mighty fast. Course I don't know about the lady."

"What don't you know about her?" asked Dick, who was by way of being both amused and pleased that the subject had been broached.

"How she feels about the proposition. She had you kicked out of the house. That looks kinder as if your show was slim. She did send over right often to see how you was getting along, but I reckon she didn't want to feel responsible for your turning up your toes. Women are that way, even when they hate a man real thorough."

"You're quite an expert. I wonder you know so much about them, and you never married."

To this sarcastic reminder Steve made philosophic reply. "Mebbe it was because I knew so much about them I never married."

"You're surely a wise old rooster. You think she hates me, then?"

Davis covered a grin. He knew from his friend's tone that the barb had pierced the skin.

"Well, looking at it like a reasonable man, there ain't any question about it. Soon as you begin to mend she quits taking any interest in you; don't know you're on the earth any more. A reasonable man—"

"A reasonable goat!" Dick reined up till the other horse was abreast of his, then dived into his pocket and handed Steve a letter. "She's quit taking any interest in me, has she? Don't know I'm on the earth, you old owl? Looks like it, and her sending me a letter this very day."

Steve turned the square envelope around and weighed it in his hand.

"Am I to read this here *billy doo*?" he wanted to know.

"Yes, sir."

Gravely the old miner opened and read the following:

"Miss Valdes begs to inform Mr. Gordon that she has reason to fear Mr. Gordon's life is not safe in the present feeling of the country. Out of regard for her people, whom she would greatly regret to see in trouble, Miss Valdes would recommend Mr. Gordon to cut short his pleasure trip to New Mexico. Otherwise Miss Valdes declines any responsibility for the result."

"Can't be called very affectionate, can it?" was Mr. Davis's comment. "Ain't it jest a leetle mite—well, like she was writing with a poker down her back?"

"I didn't say it was affectionate," snorted the young man.

"Oh, I allowed you thought she was in love with you."

"I didn't say or think anything of the kind," protested Dick indignantly. "I said she hadn't forgotten me."

"Well, she ain't, if that's any comfort."

With which, Mr. Davis handed back the letter. "What did you answer to the *billy doo*?"

"I said that Mr. Gordon presented his compliments and begged to reply that he had large business interests in this part of the country that necessitated a visit of some length, and probably in the end a permanent residence here; and that he would very fully absolve Miss Valdes of any responsibility for his remaining."

"Both of you used up a heap of dictionary words; but that wasn't so bad, either," grinned Steve. "You got back at her, all right, for the 'pleasure trip' part of her letter, but I expect you and she would disagree as to what that 'permanent residence' means. I hope it won't be more permanent than you think."

From the rocks above came the sound of an exploding rifle. Dick's hat was lifted from his head as by a gust of wind. Immediately after they caught sight of a slim, boyish figure dodging among the rocks.

"There he goes," cried Dick; and he slid from his saddle and took up the chase.

"Come back. There may be several of them up there," called the old miner.

Gordon paid no attention; and Steve had nothing left to do but follow him up the rocky hillside.

"He'll spoil that game leg of his again, first thing he knows," the old-timer growled as he followed in the rear.

Presently a second shot rang out. Davis hastened forward as fast as he could.

At the top of the ridge he came on his companion sitting behind a rock.

"Lost him in these rocks, did you?" he asked.

A sardonic smile lit up the face of his friend.

"No, Steve, I found him; but he persuaded me I oughtn't to travel so fast on this leg. You see, he had a rifle, and my six-gun was outclassed. I couldn't get into range, and decided to hunt cover, after he took another crack at me."

"I should think you'd know better than to go hunting bear with a twenty-two."

"It ain't a twenty-two; but, for a fact, it don't carry a mile. I got what I want, though. I know who the gentleman is."

"Sure it wasn't a lady, Dick?"

"Don't you, Steve," warned Gordon. "She's a lady and a Christian. You wouldn't say that if you knew her. Besides, she saved my life."

"Who was it? That Pesky fellow?"

"No. He's hot-blooded; but he wouldn't strike below the belt. He's a gentleman. This was one of the lads on her home-place, an eighteen-year-old boy named Pedro. He's in love with her. I saw it soon as I set eyes on him the day I went there. He worships her as if she were a saint. Of course, he loves her without any hope; but that doesn't keep him from being jealous of me. He's heard about the row, and he thinks he'll do her a service by putting me out of the game."

"Sort of fix you up with that permanent residence you were talking about," suggested Steve.

"He didn't make good this time, anyhow. I'll bet a hat he'd catch it if Miss Valdes knew what he had been doing."

"She may be a Christian and all you say, Dick, but she don't run a Sunday school on her ranch and train these young greasers proper. I don't like this ambushing. They might git the wrong man."

"I'm not partial to it, myself. That lead pill hummed awful close to me."

They had by this time returned to the road, and Dick picked up his hat from the dust. There were two little round holes in the crown, and one in the brim.

"If he had shot an inch lower I would have qualified for that permanent residence, Steve," Dick laughed.

"Hmp! Let's get out of here *pronto*, Dick. I'm darned if I like to be the target at a shooting gallery. And next time I go riding there's going to be a good old Winchester lying over my saddle-horn."

Now, as very chance would have it, Miss Valdes, too, rode the hill trail that afternoon; and every step of the broncos lessened the distance between them.

They met at a turn of the steep path. Davis was in the lead, and the girl passed him just in time to meet Dick's bow. It was a very respectful bow; but there was a humorous irony in the gray eyes that met hers, which hinted at a different story. She made as if to pass him, but, on an impulse, reined in. His ventilated hat came off again, as he waited for her to speak.

For an instant she let her gaze rest in his, the subdued crimson of her cheeks triumphant over the olive. But the color was not of embarrassment, and in her eyes shone the spirit of a descendant of old Don Alvaro de Valdes y Castillo. She sat her mount superbly; as jimp and erect as a willow sapling.

"You received a message from me this morning, sir," she said haughtily.

"Yes, Miss Valdes; I received a message from you this morning and answered it. This afternoon I received one from one of your friends; but I haven't answered that yet."

As he spoke he let his eyes fall upon the hat in his hand.

Hers followed his, and she started in spite of herself.

"Did—did—were you shot at?" she asked, with dilating eyes.

"Oh, well! He didn't hit me. It's not worth mentioning."

"Not worth mentioning? Who did it, sir? I demand to know who did it?"

He hesitated as he picked his words.

"You see—well—he was behind a rock, and not very close, at that."

"But you knew him. I demand his name. He shall be punished. I myself will see to that."

"I'll do what punishing needs to be done, Miss Valdes. Much obliged to you, just the same."

Her eyes flashed.

"You forget, sir, that they are my people. I gave orders—the very strictest orders. I told them that, no matter what you did or how far you went, you were not to be molested."

"How far I went? You've been served with a legal notice, then? I thought you must have by this time."

"Yes, sir, I have. But neither on that nor any other subject do I desire any conversation with you."

"Of course not, me being a spy and all those other things you mentioned," he said quietly.

"I stopped to tell you only one thing. You must leave this country. Prosecute your suit from a distance. My people are wrought up. You see for yourself now." Her gauntlet indicated the hat.

"They do seem to be enthusiastic about hating me," he agreed pleasantly. "I suppose I'm not what you would call popular here."

She gave a gesture of annoyance.

"Can't you understand that this is no time for flippancy? Can't you make him see it, sir?" she called to Davis.

That gentleman shook his head.

"He'll go his own way, I expect. He always was that bull-headed."

"Firm—I call it," smiled Gordon.

"I ask you to remember that he has had his warning," the girl called to Steve.

"I've had several," acknowledged Dick, his eyes again on the hat. "There won't be anybody to blame but myself."

"You know who shot at you. I saw it in your face. Tell me, and I will see that he is punished," she urged.

Dick shook his head imperturbably.

"No; I reckon that wouldn't do. I'm playing a lone hand. You're on the other side. How can I come and ask you to fight my battles for me? That wouldn't be playing the game. I'll attend to the young man that mistook me for a rabbit."

"Very well. As you like. But you are quite mistaken if you think I asked on your account. He had disobeyed my orders, and he deserved to pay for it. I have no further interest in the matter."

"Certainly. I understand that. What interest could Miss Valdes have in a spy and a cheat?" he drawled negligently.

The young woman flushed, made as if to speak, then turned away abruptly.

She touched her pony with the spur, and as it took the outside of the slanting, narrow trail, its hoof slipped on loose gravel and went over the edge. Dick's arm went out like a streak of lightning and caught the rein.

For an instant the issue hung in doubt whether he could hold the bronco and save her a nasty fall. The taut muscles of his lean arm and body grew rigid with the strain before the animal found its feet and the path.

"Thank you," the young woman said quietly, and at once disengaged the rein from his fingers by a turn of the pony's head.

Yet a moment, and she had disappeared round a bend in the trail. Gordon had observed with satisfaction that there had been no sign of fear in her eyes at the danger she faced, no screaming or wild clutching at his arm for help. Her word of thanks to him had been as cool and low as the rest of her talk.

"She's that game. Ain't she a thoroughbred, Steve?" demanded Dick, with deep delight in his fair foe.

"You bet she is. It's a shame for you to be annoying her this way. Why don't you come to an agreement with her?"

"She ain't ready for that yet. When the time comes I'll dictate the terms of the treaty. Don't you think it's about time for us to be heading back home?"

"Then we'll meet your lady of the ranch quicker, won't we?" chuckled Davis. "Funny you didn't think about going back till after she had passed."

But if Dick had hoped to see her again he was disappointed

for that day, at least. They reached Corbett's with never another glimpse of her; nor was there any sign of her horse in front of the post office and general store.

"Must have taken that lower trail that leads back to the ranch," hazarded Gordon.

"I reckon," agreed his friend. "Seems funny, too; her knowing you was on the upper one."

"Guy me all you like. I can stand it," returned Dick cheerfully.

For he had scored once in spite of her. He had saved her from a fall, at a place where, to say the least, it would have been dangerous. She had announced herself indifferent to his existence; but the very fact that she had felt called upon to say so gave denial to the statement. She might hate him, and she probably did; at least, she had him on her mind a good deal. The young man was sure of that. He was shrewdly of opinion that his chances were better if she hated him than if she never thought of him at all.

CHAPTER VIII

TAMING AN OUTLAW

"Something doing back of the corral, Mr. Gordon."

Yeager, the horse-wrangler at Corbett's, stopped in front of the porch, and jerked his head, with a twisted grin, in the direction indicated.

Everything about the little stableman was crooked. From the slope of his legs to the set of his bullet head on the narrow shoulders, he was awry. But he had an instinct about horses that was worth more than the beauty of any slim, tanned *vaquero* of the lot.

Only one horse had he failed to subdue. That was Teddy, a rakish sorrel that had never yet been ridden. Many had tried it, but none had stuck to the saddle to the finish; and some had been carried from the corral to the hospital.

Dick got up and strolled back, with his hands in his pockets.

A dozen *vaqueros* and loungers sat and stood around the mouth of the corral, from which a slim young Mexican was leading the sorrel.

"So, it's you, Master Pedro," thought the young American. "I didn't expect to see you here."

The lad met his eyes quietly as he passed, giving him a sullen nod of greeting; evidently he hoped he had not been recognized as the previous day's ambusher.

"Is Pedro going to ride the outcast?" Dick asked of Yeager, in surprise.

Yeager grinned.

"He's going to try. The boy's slap-up rider, but he ain't got it in him to break Teddy—no, nor any man in New Mexico ain't."

Dick looked the horse over carefully, as it stood there while the boy tightened the girths—feet wide apart, small head low, and red eyes gleaming wickedly. Deep-chested, with mighty shoulders, barrel-bodied like an Indian pony, Teddy showed power in every line of him. It was easy to guess him for the unbroken outlaw he was.

There was a swift scatter backward of the onlookers as Pedro swung to the saddle. Before his right foot was in the stirrup, the bronco bucked.

The young Mexican, light and graceful, settled to the saddle with a delighted laugh, and drove the spurs home. The animal humped like a camel, head and tail down, went into the air and back to earth, with four feet set like pile-drivers. It was a shock to drive a man's spine together like a concertina; but Pedro took it limply, giving to the jar of the impact as the pony came down again and again.

Teddy tasted the quirt along his quarters, and the pain made him frantic. He went screaming straight into the air, hung there a long instant, and fell over backward. The lad was out of the saddle in time and no more, and back in his seat before the outlaw had scrambled to his feet.

The spur starred him to renewed life. Like a flash of lightning, the brute's head swung round and snapped at the boy's leg. Pedro wrenched the head back in time to save himself; and Teddy went to sun-fishing, and presently to fence-rowing.

The dust flew in clouds. It wrapped them in so that the boy saw nothing but the wicked ears in front of him. His throat became a lime-kiln, his eyes stared like those of a man weary from long wakefulness. The hot sun baked his bare neck and head, the while Teddy rocketed into the sky and pounded into the earth.

Neither rider nor mount had mercy. The quirt went back and forth like a piston-rod, and the outlaw, in screaming fury, leaped and tossed like a small boat in a tremendous sea of cross-currents.

"It's sure hell-for-leather. That hawss can tie himself in more knots than any that was ever foaled," commented a tobacco-chewing puncher in a scarlet kerchief.

"Pedro is a straight-up rider, but he ain't got it in him to master Teddy—no; nor no man ain't," contributed Yeager again proudly. "Hawsses is like men. Some of 'em can't be broke; you can only kill them. Teddy's one of them kind."

Dick differed, but did not say so.

"Look at him now. There he goes weaving. That hawss is a devil, I tell you. He's got every hawss-trick there is, and all of 'em worked up to a combination of his own. Look out there, Ped."

The warning came too late. Teddy had jammed into the corral fence, and ground his rider's knee till the torture of the pain had distracted his attention. Once more then swept round the ugly stub nose, and the yellow teeth fastened in the leather chaps with a vicious snap that did not entirely miss the flesh of the leg.

The boy, with a cry of pain and terror, slipped to the ground, his nerve completely shaken. The sorrel lashed out with his hind feet, and missed his head by a hairbreadth. Pedro turned to run, stumbled, and went down.

The outlaw was upon him like a streak, striking with sharp chiseled forefeet at the prostrate man. Along the line of spectators ran a groan, a kind of sobbing murmur of despair. A young Mexican who had just ridden up flung himself from his horse and ran forward, though he knew he was too late.

"Pedro's done for," cried one.

And so he would have been but for the watchfulness and alertness of one man.

Dick had been ready the instant the outlaw had flung against the fence. He had been prepared to see the boy weaken, and had anticipated it in his forward leap. The furious animal had risen to drive home his hoofs, when an arm shot out, caught the bridle, and dragged him sideways. This unexpected intervention dazed the animal; and while he still stood uncertain, Gordon swung to the saddle and dug his heels into the bleeding sides.

As to a signal the bronco rose, and the battle was on again.

But this time the victory was not in doubt to the onlookers after the first half-dozen jumps. For this man rode like a master. He held a close but easy seat, and a firm rein, along which ran the message of an iron will to the sensitive foaming mouth which held the bit tight-clamped.

This brown, lithe man was all bone and sinew and muscle. He rode like a Centaur, as if he were a part of the horse, as easily and gracefully as a chip does the waves. The outlaw was furious with hate, blind with a madness that surged through it; but all its weaving and fence-rowing could not shake the perfect poise of the rider, nor tinge with fear the glad fighting edge that throbbed like a trumpet-call in the blood.

Slowly the certainty of this sifted to the animal. The pitches grew less volcanic, died presently into fitful mechanical rises and falls that foretold the finish. Its spirit broken, with that terrible incubus of a human clothes-pin still clamped to the saddle, Teddy gave up, and for the first time hung his head in token of defeat.

Dick tossed the bridle to Yeager and swung off.

"There aren't any of them so bad, if a fellow will stay with them," he said.

"Where did you learn your riding, partner?" asked the puncher with the scarlet kerchief knotted around his neck.

"I used to ride for an outfit up in Wyoming," returned Dick.

"Well, I'd like to ride for that outfit, if all the boys stick to the saddle like you," returned the kerchiefed one.

Gordon did not explain that he had been returned winner in

more than one bucking-bronco contest in the days when he rode the range.

He was already sauntering toward the house.

From a side porch Pedro, awaiting the arrival of a rig to take him back to the ranch, sat with his bruised leg on a chair and watched the approach of the stalwart figure that came as lightly as though it trod on eggs. He had hobbled here and watched the other do easily what had been beyond him.

His heart was bitter with the sense of defeat, none the less because this man whom he had lately tried to kill had just saved his life.

"*Como*?" asked Dick, stopping in front of him to brush dust from his trousers with a pocket-handkerchief.

Pedro mumbled something. Under his olive skin the color burned. Tears of mortification were in his eyes.

"You saved my life, *senor*. Take it. It is yours," the boy cried.

"What shall *I* do with it?"

"I care not. Make an end of it, as on Tuesday I tried to make an end of yours," cried the lad wildly.

Gordon took off his hat and looked at the bullet holes casually.

"You did not miss it very far, Pedro."

"You knew then, *senor*, that I was the man?" the Mexican asked in surprise.

"Oh, yes; I knew that."

"And you did nothing?"

"Yes; I ducked behind a rock," laughed Gordon.

"But you make no move to arrest me?"

"No."

"But, if I should shoot again?"

"I expect to carry a rifle next time I go riding, Pedro."

The Mexican considered this.

"You are a brave man, *senor*."

The Anglo-Saxon snorted scornfully.

"Because I ain't bluffed out by a kid that needs a horse-whip laid on good and hard? Don't you make any mistake, boy. I'm going to give you the licking of your young life. You were due for it to-day, but it will have to be postponed, I reckon, till you're on your feet again."

Pedro's eyes glittered dangerously.

"Senor Gordon has saved my life. It is his. But no living man lays hands on Pedro Menendez," the boy said, drawing himself haughtily to his full slender height.

"You'll learn better, Pedro, before the week's out. You've got to stand the gaff, just the same as a white boy would. You're in for a good whaling, and there ain't any use getting heroic about it."

"I think not, Senor Gordon." There was a suggestion of repressed emotion in the voice.

Dick turned sharply at the words. A lean, clean-built young fellow stood beside the porch. He stepped up lightly, so that he was behind the chair in which Pedro had been sitting. Seen side by side thus, there could be no mistaking the kinship between the two Mexicans. Both were good looking, both lean and muscular, both had a sort of banked volcanic passion in their black eyes. Dangerous men, these slim swarthy youths, judged Gordon with a sure instinct.

"You think not, Pedro Number 2," retorted the American lightly.

"My name is Pablo, Senor—Pablo Menendez," corrected the young man with dignity.

"Pleased to meet you, Mr. Menendez. I was just telling your brother—if Pedro is your brother—that I intend to wear out a buggy whip on him as soon as his leg is well," explained Dick pleasantly.

"No. You have saved his life. It is yours. Take it." The black eyes of the Mexican met steadily the blue-gray ones of the American.

"Much obliged, but I can't use it. As soon as I've tanned his hide I'm through with Master Pedro," returned the miner carelessly.

He was turning away when Pablo stopped him. The musical voice was low and clear. "Senor Gordon understands then. Pedro will pay. He will endure shot for shot if the Senor wishes it. But no man living shall lay a whip upon him."

Gordon shrugged his shoulders. "We shall see, my friend. The first time I meet him after his leg is all right Master Pedro gets the licking he needs."

"You are warned, *senor*."

Dick nodded and walked away, humming a song lightly.

The black eyes of the Mexicans followed him as long as he was in sight. A passionate hatred burned in those of the elder brother. Those of Pedro were full of a wistful misery. With all his heart he admired this man whom he had yesterday tried to kill, who had to-day saved his life, and in the next breath promised him a thrashing.

He gave him a grudging hero-worship, even while he hated him; for the man trod the world with the splendor of a young god, and yet was an enemy of the young mistress to whom he owed his full devotion. Pedro's mind was made up.

If this Gordon laid a whip on him, he would drive a knife into his heart.

CHAPTER IX

OF DON MANUEL AND MOONLIGHT

Don Manuel sat curled up in one of the deep window-seats of the living room at the Valdes home, and lifted his clear tenor softly in an old Spanish love-song to the accompaniment of the strumming of a guitar.

It is possible that the young Spaniard sang the serenade impersonally, as much to the elderly duenna who slumbered placidly on the other side of the fireplace as to his lovely young hostess. But his eyes told another story. They strayed continuously toward that slim, gracious figure sitting in the fireglow with a piece of embroidery in the long fingers.

He could look at her the more ardently because she was not looking at him. The fringes of her lids were downcast to the dusky cheeks, the better to examine the work upon which she was engaged.

Don Manuel felt the hour propitious. It was impossible for him not to feel that in the past weeks somehow he had lost touch with her. Something had come between them; some new interest that threatened his influence.

But to-night he had again woven the spell of romance around

　　　　　William MacLeod Raine

her. As she sat there, a sweet shadowy form touched to indistinctness by the soft dusk, he knew her gallant heart had gone with him in the Castilian battle song he had sung, had remained with him in the transition to the more tender note of love.

He rose, thumbed a chord or two, then set his guitar down softly. For a time he looked out into the valley swimming in a silvery light, and under its spell the longing in him came to words.

"It is a night of nights, my cousin. Is it not that a house is a prison in such an hour? Let us forth."

So forth they fared to the porch, and from the porch to the sentinel rock which rose like a needle from the summit of a neighboring hill. Across the sea of silver they looked to the violet mountains, soft and featureless in the lowered lights of evening, and both of them felt it earth's hour of supreme beauty.

"It is good to live—and to know this," she said at last softly.

"It is good to live and, best of all, to know you," he made answer slowly.

She did not turn from the hills, made no slightest sign that she had heard; but to herself she was saving: "It has come."

While he pleaded his cause passionately, with all the ardor of hot-blooded Spain, the girl heard only with her ears. She was searching her heart for the answer to the question she asked of it:

"*Is this the man?*"

A month ago she might have found her answer easier; but she felt that in some subtle, intangible way she was not the same girl as the Valencia Valdes she had known then. Something new had come into her life; something that at times exalted her and seemed to make life's currents sweep with more abandon.

She was at a loss to know what it meant; but, though she would not confess it even to herself, she was aware that the American was the stimulating cause. He was her enemy, and she detested him; and, in the same breath with which she would tell herself this, would come that warm beat of exultant blood she had never known till lately.

With all his ardor, Don Manuel never quickened her pulses. She liked him, understood him, appreciated his value. He was certainly very handsome, and, without doubt, a brave, courteous gentleman of her own set with whom she ought to be happy if she loved him. Ah! If she knew what love were.

So, when the torrent of Pesquiera's speech was for the moment dammed, she could only say:

"I don't know, Manuel."

Confidently he explained away her uncertainty:

"A maiden's love is retiring, shy, like the first flowers of the spring. She doubts it, fears it, hides it, my beloved, like—"

He was just swimming into his vocal stride when she cut him short decisively:

"It isn't that way with me, Manuel. I should tell you if I knew. Tell me what love is, my cousin, and I may find an answer."

He was off again in another lover's rhapsody. This time there was a smile almost of amusement in her eyes as she listened.

"If it is like that, I don't think I love you, Manuel. I don't think poetry about you, and I don't dream about you. Life isn't a desert when you are away, though I like having you here. I don't believe I care for you that way, not if love is what the poets and my cousin Manuel say it is."

Her eyes had been fixed absently now and again on an approaching wagon. It passed on the road below them, and she saw, as she looked down, that her *vaquero* Pedro lay in the bottom of it upon some hay.

"What is the matter? Are you hurt?" she called down.

The lad who was driving looked up, and flashed a row of white teeth in a smile of reassurance to his mistress.

"It is Pedro, *dona*. He tried to ride that horse Teddy, and it threw him. Before it could kill him, the *Americano* jumped in and saved his life."

"What American?" she asked quickly: but already she knew by the swift beating of her heart.

"Senor Muir; the devil fly away with him," replied the boy loyally.

Already his mistress was descending toward him with her sure stride, Don Manuel and his suit forgotten in the interest of this new development of the feud. She made the boy go over the tale minutely, asking questions sometimes when she wanted fuller details.

Meanwhile, Manuel Pesquiera waited, fuming. Most certainly

this fellow Gordon was very much in the way. Jealousy began to add its sting to the other reasons good for hastening his revenge.

When Valencia turned again to her cousin her eyes were starry.

"He is brave—this man. Is he not?" she cried.

It happened that Don Manuel, too, was a rider in a thousand. He thought that Fate had been unkind to refuse him this chance his enemy had found. But Pesquiera was a gentleman, and his answer came ungrudgingly:

"My cousin, he is a hero—as I told you before."

"But you think him base," she cried quickly.

"I let the facts speak for me," he shrugged.

"Do they condemn him—absolutely? I think not."

She was a creature of impulse, too fine of spirit to be controlled by the caution of speech that convention demands. She would do justice to her foe, no matter how Manuel interpreted it.

What the young man did think was that she was the most adorable and desirable of earth's dwellers, the woman he must win at all hazards.

"He came here a spy, under a false name. Surely you do not forget that, Valencia," he said.

"I do not forget, either, that we flung his explanations in his face; refused him the common justice of a hearing. Had we given him a chance, all might have been well."

"My cousin is generous," Manuel smiled bitterly.

"I would be just."

"Be both, my beloved, to poor Manuel Pesquiera, an unhappy wreck on the ocean of love, seeking in vain for the harbor."

"There are many harbors, Manuel, for the brave sailor. If one is closed, another is open. He hoists sail, and beats across the main to another port."

"For some. But there are others who will to one port or none. I am of those."

When she left him it was with the feeling that Don Manuel would be hard hit, if she found herself unable to respond to his love.

He was not like this American, competent, energetic, full of the turbulent life of a new nation which turns easily from defeat to fresh victory.

Her heart was full of sympathy, and even pity, for him. But these are only akin to love.

It was not long before Valencia began to suspect that she had not been told the whole truth about the affair of the outlaw horse. There was some air of mystery, of expectation, among her *vaqueros*.

At her approach, conversation became suspended, and perceptibly shifted to other topics. Moreover, Pedro was troubled in his mind, out of all proportion to the extent of his wound.

She knew it would be no use to question him; but she made occasion soon to send for Juan Gardiez, the lad who had driven him home.

From the doorway of the living-room, Juan presently ducked a bow at her.

"The *senorita* sent for me?"

"Yes. Come in, Juan. Take that chair."

Now, though Juan had often sat down in the kitchen, he had never before been invited to seat himself in this room. Wherefore, the warm smile that now met him, and went with the invitation, filled him with a more than mild surprise. Gingerly he perched himself on the edge of a chair, twirling his dusty sombrero round and round as a relief to his embarrassment.

"I am sorry, Juan, that you don't like me or trust me any longer," his mistress began.

"But, *dona*, I do," exclaimed the boy, nearly falling from his chair in amazement.

She shook her head.

"No; I can see you don't. None of you do. You keep secrets from me. You whisper and hide things."

"But, no, *senorita*—"

"Yes. I can see it plainly. My people do not love me. I must go away from them, since—"

Juan, having in his tender boyish heart a great love for his *dona*, could not stand this.

"No, no, no, *senorita*! It is not so. I do assure you it is a mistake. There is nothing about the cattle, nothing about the sheep you do not know. It is all told—all."

"*Muy bien.* Yet you conceal what happened yesterday to Pedro."

"He was thrown—"

She stopped him with a gesture.

"I don't want to know that again. Tell me what is in the air; what is planned for Senor Gordon; what Pedro has to do with it? Tell me, or leave me to know my people no longer love me."

The boy shook his head and let his eyes fall before her clear gaze.

"I can tell nothing."

"Look at me, Juan," she commanded, and waited till he obeyed. "Pedro it was that shot at this man Gordon. Is it not so?"

His eyes grew wide.

"Some one has told?" he said questioningly.

"No matter. It was he. Yesterday the American saved his life. Surely Pedro does not still—"

She did not finish in words, but her eyes chiseled into his

stolid will to keep silent.

"The stranger invites evil. He would rob the *senorita* and us all. He has said he would horsewhip Pedro. He rides up and down the valley, taunting us with his laugh. Is he a god, and are we slaves?"

"He said he would horsewhip Pedro, did he?"

"*Si senorita*; when Pedro told him to take his life, since it was his."

"And this was after Pedro had been thrown?"

"Directly after. The American is a devil, *dona*. He rode that man-killer like Satan. Did he not already know that it was Pedro who shot at him? Is not Pedro a sure shot, and did he not miss twice? Twice, *senorita*; which makes it certain that this *Senor* Gordon is a devil."

"Don't talk nonsense, Juan. I want to know how he came to tell Pedro that he would whip him."

"He came up to the piazza when he had broken the heart of that other devil, the man-killer, and Pedro was sitting there. Then Pedro told him that he was the one who had shot at him, but he only laughed. He always laughs, this fiend. He knew it already, just as he knows everything. Then it was he said he had saved the boy to whip him."

"And that is all?"

"*Por Dios*—all" shrugged the lad.

"Are there others beside you that believe this nonsense about the American being in league with evil?"

"It is not nonsense, *senorita*, begging your pardon," protested Juan earnestly. "And Ferdinand and Pablo and Sebastian, they all believe it."

Valencia knew this complicated the situation. These simple peons would do, under the impulsion of blind bigotry, what they would hesitate to do otherwise. Let them think him a devil, and they would stick at nothing to remove him.

Her first thought was that she must keep informed of the movements of her people. Otherwise she would not be able to frustrate them.

"Juan, if this man is really what you think, he will work magic to destroy those who oppose him. It will not be safe for any of my people to set themselves against him. I know a better way to attack him. I want to talk with Pablo and Sebastian. You must work with me. If they try to do anything, let me know at once; otherwise they will be in great danger. Do you understand?"

"*Si, senorita.*"

"And will you let me know, quietly, without telling them?"

"*Si, senorita.*"

"That is good. Now, I know my Juan trusts and loves his mistress. You have done well. Go, now."

From the point of view of her people the girl knew it was all settled. If the stranger whipped Pedro, the boy would kill him unless he used magic to prevent it. If he did use it, they must contrive to nullify his magic. There, too, Don Manuel, who would surely strike soon, and however the encounter might terminate, it was a thing to dread miserably.

But, though her misery was acute, she was of a temperament too hopeful and impulsive to give up to despair so long as action was possible. While she did not yet know what she could do, she was not one to sit idle while events hurried to a crisis.

Meantime she had her majordomo order a horse saddled for her to ride over to Corbett's for the mail.

CHAPTER X

MR. AINSA DELIVERS A MESSAGE

Back to Davis, who had stopped to tighten his saddle-girth, came Dick Gordon's rather uncertain tenor in rollicking song:

> "Bloomin' idol made o' mud—
> Wot they called the Great Gawd Budd—
> Plucky lot she cared for idols when I
> Kissed 'er where she stud!"

"There he goes, advertising himself for a target to every greaser in the county. Pity he can't ride along decent, if he's got to ride at all in these hills, where every gulch may be a trap," grumbled the old miner.

He jerked the leather strap down with a final tug, pulled himself to the saddle, and cantered after his friend.

> "Elephints a pilin' teak
> In the sludgy, squdgy creek,
> Where the silence 'ung that 'eavy you
> Was 'arf afraid to speak!"

"No danger of the silence hanging heavy here while you're

around trying to be a whole opery troupe all by your lonesome," suggested Davis. "Seems to me if you got to trapse round this here country hunting for that permanent residence, it ain't necessary to disturb the Sabbath calm so on-feelin'. I don't seem to remember hearing any great demand for an encore after the rendering of the first verse."

"You do ce'tainly remind me of a lien with one chick, Steve," laughed Dick.

"I ain't worrying about you none. It's my own scalp kinder hangs loose every time you make one of your fool-plays," explained the other.

"Go pipe that up to your granny. Think I ain't learned my ABC's about my dry-nurse yet?"

"I'm going back to the gold camp to-morrow."

"You been saying that ever since you came here. Why don't you go, old Calamity Prophet?"

"Well, I am. Going to-morrow."

"You've hollered wolf too often, Steve. I'll believe it when I see it."

"Well, why don't you behave? What's the use of making a holy Caruso of yourself? Nobody ain't ever pined to hear you tune up, anyhow."

"All right. Mum's the word, old hoss. I'll be as solemn as if I was going to my own funeral."

"I ain't persuaded yet you're not."

"I'm right fully persuaded. Hallo! Stranger visiting at Corbett's. Guess I'll unlimber the artillery."

They dismounted, and, before turning over his horse to Yeager, Dick unstrapped from the saddle his rifle. Nowadays he never for a moment was separated from some weapon of defense. For he knew that an attack upon his life was almost a certainty in the near future. Though his manner was debonair, he saw to it that nobody got a chance to tamper with his guns.

"Make you acquainted with Mr. Ramon Ainsa, gentlemen. Mr. Gordon—Mr. Davis," said Corbett, standing in the doorway in his shirt-sleeves.

Mr. Ainsa, a very young man with the hint of a black mustache over his boyish mouth, clicked his heels together and bowed deeply. He expressed himself as delighted, but did not offer to shake hands. He was so stiff that Dick wanted to ask him whether the poker he had swallowed was indigestible.

"I am the bearer of a message to Mr. Richard Muir Gordon," he said with another bow.

"My name," acknowledged its owner. "You ain't missed a letter of it. Must have been at the christening, I expect."

"A message from Don Manuel Pesquiera."

"Good enough. That's right friendly of him. How's the *don*?"

And Dick, the sparkle of malicious humor gleaming in his eye, shook Mr. Ainsa warmly by the hand, in spite of that gentleman's effort to escape.

The messenger sidestepped as soon as he could, and began again, very red:

"Don Manuel considers himself deeply insulted, and desires through me, his friend, to present this note."

Dick looked at the envelope, and back at the youth who had handed it to him, after which he crowded in and pump-handled the other's arm again.

"That's awfully good of him, Mr. 'Tain't-so."

"My name is Ainsa, at your service," corrected the New Mexican.

"Beg pardon—Ainsa. I expect I hadn't ought to have irrigated the *don* so thorough, but it's real good of him to overlook it and write me a friendly note. It's uncommon handsome of him after I disarranged his laundry so abrupt."

"If the *senor* will read the letter—" interrupted the envoy desperately.

"Certainly. But let me offer you something to drink first, Mr. Ain't-so."

"Ainsa."

"Ainsa, I should say. A plain American has to go some to round up and get the right brand on some of these blue-blooded names of yours. What'll it be?"

"Thank you. I am not thirsty. I prefer not." With which Mr. Ainsa executed another bow.

"Just as you say, colonel. But you'll let me know if you

change your mind."

Dick indicated a chair to his visitor, and took another himself; then leisurely opened the epistle and read it. After he had done so he handed it to Davis.

"This is for you, too, Steve. The *don* is awfully anxious to have you meet Mr. Ainsa and have a talk with him," chuckled Gordon.

"'To arrange a meeting with your friend,' Why, it's a duel he means, Dick."

"That's what I gathered. We're getting right up in society. A duel's more etiquettish than bridge-whist, Steve. Ain't you honored, being invited to one. You're to be my second, you see."

"I'm hanged if I do," exploded the old miner promptly.

"Sho! It ain't hard, when you learn the steps."

"I ain't going to have nothing to do with it. Tommyrot! That's what I call it."

"Don't say it so loud, Steve, or you'll hurt Mr. Ainsa's feelings," chided his partner.

"Think I'm going to make a monkey of myself at my age?"

Dick turned mournfully to the messenger of war.

"I'm afraid it's off, Mr. Ainsa. My second says he won't play."

"We shall be very glad to furnish you a second, sir."

"All right, and while you're at it furnish a principal, too. I'm an American. I write my address Cripple Creek, Colorado, U.S.A. We don't fight duels in my country any more. They've gone out with buckled shoes and knee-pants, Mr. Ainsa."

"Do I understand that Mr. Gordon declines to meet my friend on the field of honor?"

"That's the size of it."

"I am then instruct' to warn you to go armed, as my friend will punish your insolence at sight informally."

It was just at this moment that Mrs. Corbett, flushed with the vain chase of her fleeing brood of chickens, came perspiring round the house. Her large, round person, not designed by nature for such arduous exercise, showed signs of fatigue.

"I declare, if them chickens ain't got out, and me wanting two for supper," she panted, arms on her ample hips.

"That's too bad. Let me chase them," volunteered Dick.

He grasped his rifle, took a quick, careless aim, and fired. A long-legged, flying cockerel keeled over and began to kick.

"Gracious me!" ejaculated the woman.

"Two, did you say?" asked the man behind the gun.

"I said two."

Again the rifle cracked. A second chicken flopped down, this one with its head shot off at the neck.

The eyes of the minister of war were large with amazement. The distance had been seventy yards, if it had been a step. When little Jimmie Corbett came running forward with the two dead cockerels a slight examination showed that the first had also been shot through the neck.

Dick smiled.

"Shall I shoot another and send it for a present to Don Manuel, Jimmie?" he pleasantly inquired.

Mr. Ainsa met his persiflage promptly.

"I do assure you, *senor*, it will not be at all necesair. Don Manuel can shoot chickens for himself—and larger game."

"I'm sure he'll find good hunting," the other gave him back, looking up genially.

"He is a good hunter, *senor*."

"Don't doubt it a bit," granted the cordial Anglo-Saxon. "Trouble is that even the best hunters can't tell whether they are going to bring back the bear, or Mr. Bear is going to get them. That's what makes it exciting, I reckon."

"Is Don Manuel going bear-hunting?" asked Jimmie, with a newly aroused boy interest.

"Yes, Jimmie. One's been bothering him right considerable, and he's going gunning for it," explained Dick.

"Gee! I hope he gets it."

"And I hope he don't," laughed Gordon. "Must you really be going, colonel? Can't I do a thing for you in the refreshment line first? Well, so long. Good hunting for your friend. See him later."

Thus cheerfully did the irrepressible Gordon speed Mr. Ainsa on his way.

That young man had somehow the sense of having been too youthful to cope with the gay Gordon.

* * * * *

Valencia Valdes had not ridden far when she met Ramon Ainsa returning from his mission. He was a sunny young fellow, whom she had known since they had been children together.

It occurred to her that he bore himself in a manner that suggested something important on hand. His boyish mouth was set severely, and he greeted her with a punctilio quite unusual. At once she jumped shrewdly to a conclusion.

"Did you bring our mail back with you from Corbett's?" she innocently inquired.

"Yes, *senorita.*"

"Since when have I been '*senorita*' to you, Ramon?"

"Valencia, I should say." He blushed.

"Indeed, I should think so. It hasn't been so long since you called me Val."

"Ah! Those happy days!" he sighed.

"Fiddlesticks!" she promptly retorted. "Don't be a goose.

You're not in the sere and yellow yet. Don't forget you'll not be twenty-one till next month."

"One counts time not by years, but by its fullness," he said, in the manner of one who could tell volumes if he would.

"I see. And what has been happening of such tremendous importance?"

Mr. Ainsa attempted to twirl his mustache, and was as silent as honor demanded.

"Pooh! It's no secret. Did you find Mr. Gordon at home?"

"At home?" he gasped.

"Well, at Corbett's, then?"

"I didn't know—Who told you—er—"

"I'm not blind and deaf and dumb, you know."

"But you certainly have a great deal of imagination," he said, recovering himself.

"Not a bit of it. You carried a challenge to this American from Don Manuel. Now, I want to know the answer."

"Really, my dear girl—"

"You needn't try to evade me. I'm going to know, if I stay here all night."

"It's a hold-up, as the Americans say," he joked.

"I don't care what you call it. You have got to tell me,

you know."

"But I can't tell you, *nina*. It isn't mine to tell."

"Anyhow, you can't keep me from guessing," she said, with an inspiration.

"No, I don't see how I can very well," he admitted.

"The American accepted the challenge immediately."

"But he didn't," broke out the young man.

"Then he refused?"

"That's a little obvious now," replied Ramon, with a touch of chagrin.

"He was very angry about it, and threatened to call the law to his aid."

Her friend surrendered at discretion, and broke into a laugh of delight.

"I never saw such a fellow, Val. He seemed to think it was all a joke. He must have known why I was there, but before I could get in a word he got hold of my hand and shook it till I wanted to shriek with the pain. He's got a grip like a bear. And he persisted in assuming we were the best of friends. Wouldn't read the letter at all."

"But after he did?"

"Said duels were not fashionable among his people any more."

"He is very sensible, but I'm afraid Manuel won't rest satisfied with that," the girl sighed.

"I hinted as much, and told him to go armed. What do you think the madman did then?"

"I can never guess."

Ramon retailed the chicken-shooting episode.

"You were to mention that to Manuel, I suppose?'" the girl said thoughtfully.

"So I understood. He was giving fair warning."

"But Manuel won't be warned."

"When he hears of it he'll be more anxious than ever to fight."

Valencia nodded. "A spur to a willing horse."

"If he knew he would be killed it would make no difference to him. He is quite fearless."

"Quite."

"But he is a very good shot, too. You do not need to be alarmed for him."

"Oh, no! Not at all," the girl answered scornfully. "He is only my distant cousin, anyhow—and my lover."

"It is hard, Val. Perhaps I might pick a quarrel with this American and—"

She caught him up sharply, but he forgave it when he saw her white misery.

"Don't you dare think of it, Ramon Ainsa. One would think nobody in the valley had any business except fighting with this man. What has he done to you? Or to these others? You are very brave, all of you, when you know you are a hundred to one. I suppose *you*, too, will want to shoot him from ambush?"

This bit of feminine injustice hurt the young man, but he only said quietly:

"No; I don't think I would do that."

Impulsively she put out her hand.

"Forgive me, Ramon. I don't mean that, of course, but I'm nearly beside myself. Why must all this bad will and bloodshed come into our happy little valley? If we must have trouble why can't we let the law settle it? I thought you were my friends—you and Manuel and my people—but between you I am going to be made unhappy for life."

She broke down suddenly and began to sob. The lad slipped to the ground and went quickly to her, putting an arm around her waist across the saddle.

"Don't cry, Val. We all love you—of course we do. How can we help it? It will all come right yet. Don't cry, *nina*"

"How can it come right, with all of you working to make things wrong?" she sobbed.

"Perhaps the stranger will go away."

"He won't. He is a man, and he won't let you drive him out."

"We'll find some way, Val, to save Manuel for you."

"But it isn't only Manuel. I don't want any of you hurt—you or anybody—not even this Mr. Gordon. Oh, Ramon, help me to stop this wicked business."

"If you can tell me how."

She dabbed her eyes with a handkerchief, as a sign that her weakness was past.

"We must find a way. Do you know, my own people are in a dangerous mood? They think this man's some kind of a demon. I shall talk to them to-night. And you must send Manuel to me. Perhaps he may listen to me."

Ainsa agreed, though he felt sure that even she could not induce his friend to withdraw from a position which he felt his honor called him to take.

Nor did the mistress of the valley find it easy to lead her tenants to her way of thinking. They were respectful, outwardly acquiescent, but the girl saw, with a sinking heart, that they remained of their own opinion. Whether he were man or devil, they were determined to make an end of Gordon's intrusion.

CHAPTER XI

THE SIXTEENTH CENTURY
AND THE TWENTIETH

It was the second day after Pesquiera's challenge that his rival was called to Santa Fe, the capital of the State, to hold a conference with his lawyers about the progress of the suit of ouster against those living on the Moreno grant. Gordon knew how acute was the feeling of the residents of the valley against him. The Corbetts, whose homestead was not included in either the original Valdes or Moreno grant, reported daily to him whatever came to their ears. He could see that the impression was strong among the Mexicans that their champion, Dona Maria as they called her, would be worsted in the courts if the issue ever came to final trial.

To live under the constant menace of an attack from ambush is a strain upon the best of nerves. Dick and his friend Davis rode out of the valley to meet the Santa Fe stage with a very sensible relief. For a few days, anyhow, they would be back where they could see the old Stars and Stripes flutter, where feudal retainers and sprouts of Spanish aristocracy were not lying in wait with fiery zeal to destroy the American interloper.

They reached the little city late, but soon after sunup Gordon rose, took a bath, dressed, and strolled out into the quaint old town which lays claim to being the earliest permanent European settlement in the country. It was his first visit to the place, and as he poked his nose into out of the way corners Dick found every step of his walk interesting.

Through narrow, twisted streets he sauntered, along unpaved roads bounded by century-old adobe houses. His walk took him past the San Miguel Church, said to be the oldest in America. A chubby-faced little priest was watering some geraniums outside, and he showed Dick through the mission, opening the door of the church with one of a bunch of large keys which hung suspended from his girdle. The little man went through the usual patter of the guide with the facility of long practice.

The church was built, he said, in 1540, though Bandelier inaccurately sets the date much later. The roof was destroyed by the Pueblo Indians in 1680 during an attack upon the settlement, at which time the inhabitants took refuge within the mission walls. These are from three to five feet thick. The arrows of the natives poured through the windows. The senor could still see the holes in the pictures, could he not? Penuelo restored the church in 1710, as could be read by the inscription carved upon the gallery beam. It would no doubt interest the senor to know that one of the paintings was by Cimabue, done in 1287, and that the seven hundred pound bell was cast in Spain during the year 1356 and had been dragged a thousand miles across the deserts of the new world by the devoted pioneer priests who carried the Cross to the simple natives of that region.

Gordon went blinking out of the San Miguel mission into a world that basked indolently in a pleasant glow of sunshine. It seemed to him that here time had stood still. This impression remained with him during his tramp back to the hotel. He passed trains of faggot-laden burros, driven by

Mexicans from Tesuque and by Indians from adjoining villages, the little animals so packed around their bellies with firewood that they reminded him of caricatures of beruffed Elizabethan dames of the olden days.

Surely this old town, which seemed to be lying in a peaceful siesta for centuries unbroken, was an unusual survival from the buried yesterdays of history. It was hard to believe, for instance, that the Governor's Palace, a long one-story adobe structure stretching across one entire side of the plaza, had been the active seat of so much turbulent and tragic history, that for more than three hundred years it had been occupied continuously by Spanish, Mexican, Indian, and American governors. Its walls had echoed the noise of many a bloody siege and hidden many an execution and assassination. From this building the old Spanish cavaliers Onate and Vicente de Salivar and Penalosa set out on their explorations. From it issued the order to execute forty-eight Pueblo prisoners upon the plaza in front. Governor Armijo had here penned his defiance to General Kearney, who shortly afterward nailed upon the flagpole the Stars and Stripes. The famous novel "Ben Hur" was written in one of these historic rooms.

But the twentieth century had leaned across the bridge of time to shake hands with the sixteenth. A new statehouse had been built after the fashion of new Western commonwealths, and the old Palace was now given over to curio stores and offices. Everywhere the new era compromised with the old. He passed the office of the lawyer he had come to consult, and upon one side of the sign ran the legend:

Despacho
De
Thomas M. Fitt, Licendiado.

Upon the other he read an English translation:

Law Office
of
Thomas M. Fitt, Attorney.

Plainly the old civilization was beginning to disappear before an alert, aggressive Americanism.

At the hotel the modern spirit became so pronounced during breakfast, owing to the conversation of a shoe and a dress-goods drummer at an adjoining table, that Gordon's imagination escaped from the tramp of Spanish mailclad cavalry and from thoughts of the plots and counterplots that had been devised in the days before American occupancy.

In the course of the morning Dick, together with Davis, called at the office of his attorney. Thomas M. Fitt, a bustling little man with a rather pompous manner, welcomed his client effusively. He had been appointed local attorney in charge by Gordon's Denver lawyers, and he was very eager to make the most of such advertising as his connection with so prominent a case would bring.

He washed the backs of his hands with the palms as he bowed his visitors to chairs.

"I may say that the case is progressing favorably—very favorably indeed, Mr. Gordon. The papers have been drawn and filed. We await an answer from the defendants. I anticipate that there will be only the usual court delays in pressing the action."

"We'll beat them, I suppose," Dick replied, with a manner

almost of indifference.

"One can never be positive in advance, but I'd like to own your claim to the estate, Mr. Gordon," laughed the lawyer wheezily.

"Think we'll be able to wolf the real owners out of their property all right, do you?"

Fitt's smile went out like the flame of a burnt match. The wrinkles of laughter were ironed out of his fat cheeks. He stared at his client in surprise. It took him a moment to voice the dignified protest he felt necessary.

"Our title is good in law, Mr. Gordon. I have been over the evidence very carefully. The court decisions all lean our way. Don Bartolome Valdes, the original grantee, failed to perfect his right of ownership in many ways. It is very doubtful whether he himself had not before his death abandoned his claim. His official acts appear to point to that conclusion. Our case is a very substantial one—very substantial, indeed."

"The Valdes' tenants have settled on the land, grazed their flocks over it, bought farms here and there from the heirs, haven't they?"

"Exactly. But if the sellers cannot show a good title—and my word as a lawyer for it they can't. Prove that in court and all we'll need is a writ of ejectment against the present holders as squatters. Then—" Fitt snapped his finger and thumb in an airy gesture that swept the Valdes' faction into the middle of the Pacific.

"It'll be the story of Evangeline all over again, won't it?" asked Gordon satirically.

"Ah! You have a kind heart, Mr. Gordon. Your sympathy does you credit. Still—business is business, of course."

"Of course," Dick picked up a pen and began to jab holes aimlessly into a perfectly good blotter tacked to the table. "Well, let's hear the story—just a sketch of it. Why do the rightful heirs lose out and the villain gain possession?"

Mr. Fitt smiled blandly. He had satisfied himself that his client was good pay and he did not intend to take offense. "It pleases you to be facetious, Mr. Gordon. But we all know that what this country needs—what such a valley as the Rio Chama ought to have—is up to date American development. People and conditions are in a primitive state. When men like you get possession of the Moreno and similar tracts New Mexico will move forward with giant strides to its great destiny. Time does not stand still. The day of the indolent semi-feudal Spanish system of occupancy has passed away. New Mexico will no longer remain *manana* land. You—and men like you—of broad ideas, progressive, energetic—"

"Quite a philanthropist, ain't I?" interrupted Gordon, smiling lazily. "Well, let's hear the yarn, Mr. Fitt."

The attorney gave up his oration regretfully. He subsided into a chair and resumed the conversational tone.

"You've got to understand how things were here in the old Spanish days, gentlemen. Don Bartolome for instance was not merely a cattleman. He was a grandee, a feudal lord, a military chief to all his tenants and employees. His word was law. The power of life and death lay in him."

Dick nodded. "Get you."

"The old Don was pasturing his sheep in the Rio Chama

valley and he had started a little village there—called the place Torreon, I think, from a high tower house he had built to overlook the valley so that Indians could be seen if they attempted an attack. Well, he takes a notion that he'd better get legal title to the land he was using, though in those days he might have had half of New Mexico for his cattle and sheep as a range. So he asks Facundo Megares, governor of the royal province, for a grant of land. The governor, anxious to please him, orders the constitutional alcalde, a person named Jose Garcia de la Mora, to execute the act of possession to Valdes of a tract described as follows, to wit—"

"I've heard the description," cut in the young man. "Well, did the Don take possession?"

"We claim that he never did. He visited there, and his shepherds undoubtedly ran sheep on the range covered by the grant. But Valdes and his family never actually resided on the estate. Other points that militate against the claim of his descendants may be noted. First, that minor grants of land, taken from within the original Valdes grant, were made by the governor without any protest on the part of the Don. Second, that Don Bartolome himself, subsequently Governor and Captain-General of the province of New Mexico, did, in his official capacity as President of the Council, endorse at least two other small grants of land cut out from the heart of the Valdes estate. This goes to show that he did not himself consider that he owned the land, or perhaps he felt that he had forfeited his claim."

"Or maybe it just showed that the old gentleman was no hog," suggested Gordon.

"I guess the law will construe it as a waiver of his claim. It doesn't make any allowances for altruism."

"I've noticed that," Gordon admitted dryly.

"A new crowd of politicians got in after Mexico became independent of Spain. The plums had to be handed out to the friends of the party in power. So Manuel Armijo, the last Mexican Governor of the province, being a favorite of the President of that country because he had defeated some Texas Rangers in a battle, and on that account endowed with extraordinary powers, carved a fat half million acres out of the Valdes grant and made a present of it to Jose Moreno for 'services to the government of Mexico.' That's where you come in as heir to your grandfather, who purchased for a song the claim of Moreno's son."

"My right has been lying dormant twenty-five years. Won't that affect its legality?"

"No. If we knock out the Valdes' grant, all we have to do is to prove the legality of the Moreno one. It happens we have evidence to show that he satisfied all legal requirements by living on the land more than four years. This gave him patent in perpetuity subject to taxes. By the payment of these we can claim title." Fitt rubbed his hands and walked backward and forward briskly. "We've got them sewed up tight, Mr. Gordon. The Supreme Court has sustained our contention in the almost parallel Baca case."

"Fine," said Dick moodily. He knew it was unreasonable for him to be annoyed at his counsel because the latter happened to be an alert and competent lawyer. But somehow all his sympathies were with Valencia Valdes and her dependents.

"If you'd like to look at the original documents in the case, Mr. Gordon—"

"I would."

"I'll take you up to the State House this afternoon. You can look over them at your leisure."

Davis laughed at his friend as they walked back to the hotel.

"I don't believe you know yourself what you want. You act as if you'd rather lose than win the suit."

"Sometimes I'm a white man, Steve. I don't want to grab other people's property just because some one can dig up a piece of paper that says it's mine. We sit back and roast the trusts to a fare-you-well for hogging all there is in sight. That's what Fitt and his tribe expect me to do. I'm damned if I will."

CHAPTER XII

"I BELIEVE YOU'RE IN LOVE WITH HER, TOO"

It was characteristic of Dick Gordon that he established at once a little relation of friendliness between him and the young woman at the State House who waited upon him with the documents in the Valdes grant case. She was a tall, slight girl with amazingly vivid eyes set in a face scarcely pretty. In her manner to the world at large there was an indifference amounting almost to insolence. She had a way of looking at people as if they were bits of the stage setting instead of individuals.

A flare of interest had sparkled in her eyes when Gordon's fussy little attorney had mentioned the name of his client, but it had been Dick's genial manner of boyish comradeship that had really warmed Miss Underwood to him. She did not like many people, but when she gave her heart to a friend it was without stipulations. Dick was a man's man. Essentially he was masculine, virile, dominant. But the force of him was usually masked either by his gay impudence or his sunny friendliness. Women were drawn to his flashing smile because they sensed the strength behind it.

Kate Underwood could have given a dozen reasons why she liked him. There were for instance the superficial ones. She liked the way he tossed back the tawny sun-kissed hair from his eyes, the easy pantherish stride with which he covered ground so lightly, the set of his fine shoulders, the peculiar tint of his lean, bronzed cheeks. His laugh was joyous as the song of a bird in early spring. It made one want to shout with him. Then, too, she tremendously admired his efficiency. To look at the hard, clear eye, at the clean, well-packed build of the man, told the story. The movements of his strong, brown hands were sure and economical. They dissipated no energy. Every detail of his personality expressed a mind that did its own thinking swiftly and incisively.

"It's curious about these documents of the old Valdes and Moreno claims. They have lain here in the vaults—that is, here and at the old Governor's Palace—for twenty years and more untouched. Then all at once twenty people get interested in them. Scarce a day passes that lawyers are not up to look over some of the copies. You have certainly stirred things up with your suit, Mr. Gordon."

Dick looked out of the window at the white adobe-lined streets resting in a placid coma of sun-beat.

"Don't you reckon Santa Fe can stand a little stirring up, Miss Underwood?"

"Goodness, yes. We all get to be three hundred years old if we live in this atmosphere long enough."

The man's gaze shifted. "You'd have to live here a right long time, I reckon."

A quick slant of her gay eyes reproached him. "You don't have to be so gallant, Mr. Gordon. The State pays me fifteen hundred dollars a year to wait on you, anyhow."

"You don't say. As much as that? My, we're liable to go bankrupt in New Mexico, ain't we? And, if you want to know, I don't say nice things to you because I have to, but because I want to."

She laughed with a pretense at incredulity. "In another day or two I'll find out just what special favor I'm able to do Mr. Gordon. The regular thing is to bring flowers or candy, you know. Generally they say, too, that there never has been a clerk holding this job as fit for it as I am."

"You're some clerk, all right. Say, where can I find the original of this *Agua Caliente* grant, Miss Kate?"

She smiled to herself as she went to get him a certified copy. "Only two days, and he's using my first name. Inside of a week he'll be calling me 'Dearie,'" she thought. But she knew very well there was no danger. This young fellow was the kind of man that could be informal without the slightest idea of flirting or making love.

Kate Underwood's interest in the fight between the claimants for the Valdes and Moreno grants was not based entirely upon her liking for Dick. He learned this the fourth day of his stay in Santa Fe.

"Do you know that you were followed to the hotel last night, Mr. Gordon?" she asked him, as soon as he arrived at the State House.

His eyes met hers instantly. "Was I? How do you know?"

"I left the building just after you did. Two Mexicans followed you. I don't know when I first suspected it, but I trailed along to make sure. There can be no doubt about it."

"Not a bit of doubt. Found it out the first day when I left the hotel," he told her cheerfully.

"You knew it all the time," she cried, amazed.

"That doesn't prevent me from being properly grateful to you for your kindness," he hastened to say.

"What are they following you for?" she wanted to know.

Dick told her something of his experiences in the Rio Chama Valley without mentioning that part of them which had to do with Miss Valdes. At the sound of Manuel Pesquiera's name the eyes of the girl flashed. Dick had already noticed that his name was always to her a signal for repression of some emotion. The eyes contracted and hardened the least in the world. Some men would not have noticed this, but more than once Gordon's life had hung upon the right reading of such signs.

"You think that Mr. Pesquiera has hired them to watch you?" she suggested.

"Maybe he has and maybe he hasn't. Some of those willing lads of Miss Valdes don't need any hiring. They want to see what I'm up to. They're not overlooking any bets."

"But they may shoot you."

He looked at her drolly. "They may, but I'll be there at the time. I'm not sleeping on the job, Miss Kate."

"You didn't turn around once yesterday."

"Hmp! I saw them out of the edge of my eyes. And when I turned a corner I always saw them mighty plain. They couldn't have come very close without my knowing it."

"Don Manuel is very anxious to have Miss Valdes win, isn't he?"

Dick observed that just below the eyes two spots were burning in the usually pale cheeks.

"Yes," he answered simply.

"Why?"

"He's her friend and a relative."

It seemed to Gordon that there was a touch of defiance in the eyes that held to his so steadily. She was going to find out the truth, no matter what he thought.

"Is that all—nothing more than a friend or a relative?"

The miner's boyish laugh rippled out. "You'd ought to have been a lawyer, Miss Kate. No, that ain't all Don Manuel doesn't make any secret of it. I don't know why I should. He wants to be prince consort of the Valdes kingdom."

"Because of... the estate?"

"Lord, no! He's one man from the ground up, M. Pesquiera is. In spite of the estates."

"You mean that he... loves Valencia Valdes?"

"Sure he does. Manuel doesn't care much who gets the kingdom if he gets the princess."

"Is she so... pretty?"

Dick stopped to consider this. "Why, yes, I reckon she is pretty, though I hadn't thought of it before. You see, pretty ain't just the word. She's a queen. That is, she looks like a queen ought to but don't. Take her walk for instance: she steps out like as if in another moment she might fly."

"That doesn't mean anything. It's almost silly," replied the downright Miss Underwood, not without a tinge of spite.

"It means something to me. I'm trying to give you a picture of her. But you'd have to see her to understand. When she's around mean and little things crawl out of your mind. She's on the level and square and fine—a thoroughbred if there ever was one."

"I believe you're in love with her, too."

The young man found himself blushing. "Now don't get to imagining foolishness. Miss Valdes hates the ground I walk on. She thinks I'm the limit, and she hasn't forgotten to tell me so."

"Which, of course, makes you fonder of her," scoffed Miss Underwood. "Does she hate the ground that Don Manuel walks on?"

"Now you've got me. I go to the foot of the class, because I don't know."

"But you wish you did," she flung at him, with a swift side glance.

"Guessing again, Miss Kate. I'll sure report you if you waste the State's time on such foolishness," he threatened gaily.

"Since you're in love with her, why don't you marry Miss

Valdes and consolidate the two claims?" demanded the girl.

Her chin was tilted impudently toward him, but Gordon guessed that there was an undercurrent of meaning in her audacity.

"What commission do you charge for running your matrimonial bureau?" he asked innocently.

"The service comes free to infants," she retorted sweetly.

She was called away to attend to other business. An hour later she passed the desk where he was working.

"So you think I'm an infant at that game, do you?"

"I didn't mean to hurt your feelings," was her saucy answer.

"You haven't—not a mite. What about Don Manuel? Is he an infant at it, too?"

A sudden flame of color swept her face. The words she flung at Gordon seemed irrelevant, but he did not think them so. "I hate him."

And with that she was gone.

Dick's eyes twinkled. He had discovered another reason for her interest in his fortunes.

Later in the day, when the pressure of work had relaxed, the clerk drifted his way again while searching for some papers.

"Your lawyers are paid to look up all this, aren't they? Why do you do it, then?" she asked.

"The case interests me. I want to know all about it."

"Would you like to see the old Valdes house here in Santa Fe? My father bought it when Alvaro Valdes built his new town house. One day I found in the garret a bundle of old Spanish letters. They were written by old Bartolome to his son. I saved them. Would you care to see them?"

"Very much. The old chap was a great character. I suppose he was really the last of the great feudal barons. The French Revolution put an end to them in Europe—that and the industrial revolution. It's rather amazing that out here in the desert of this new land dedicated to democracy the idea was transplanted and survived so long."

"I'll bring the letters to-morrow and you can look them over. Any time you like I'll show you over the house. It's really rather interesting—much more so than their new one, which is so modern that it looks like a thousand others. Valencia was born in the old house. What will you give me to let you into the room?"

He brushed aside her impudence with a laugh. "Your boss is looking this way. I think he's getting ready to fire you."

"He's more likely to be fired himself. I'm under civil service and he isn't. Will you take your shoes off when you go into the holy of holies?"

"What happens to little girls when they ask too many questions? Go 'way. I'm busy."

CHAPTER XIII

AMBUSHED

On her return from luncheon that same afternoon Miss Underwood brought Dick a bundle of letters tied with a ribbon. She tossed them down upon the desk in front of him.

"I haven't read them myself. Of course they're in Spanish. I did try to get through one of them, but it was too much like work and I gave it up. But since they're written by *her* grandfather they'll interest you more than they did me," Miss Kate told him, with the saucy tilt to her chin that usually accompanied her impudence.

He had lived in Chihuahua three years as a mining engineer, so that he spoke and read Spanish readily. The old Don wrote a stiff angular hand, but as soon as he became accustomed to it Dick found little difficulty. Some of the letters were written from the ranch, but most of them carried the Santa Fe date line at the time the old gentleman was governor of the royal province. They were addressed to his son Alvaro, at that time a schoolboy in Mexico City. Clearly Don Bartolome intended his son to be informed as to the affairs of the province, for the letters were a mine of information in regard to political and social conditions. They discussed at length, too, the business interests of the family and the welfare of the peons dependent upon it.

All afternoon Gordon pored over these fascinating pages torn from a dead and buried past. They were more interesting than any novel he had ever read, for they gave him a photograph, as it were projected by his imagination upon a moving picture canvas, of the old regime that had been swept into the ash heap by modern civilization. The letters revealed the old Don frankly. He was proud, imperious, heady, and intrepid. To his inferiors he was curt but kind. They flocked to him with their troubles and their quarrels. The judgment of their overlord was final with his tenants. Clearly he had a strong sense of his responsibilities to them and to the state. A quaint flavor of old-world courtesy ran through the letters like a thread of gold.

It was a paragraph from one of the last letters that riveted Dick's attention. Translated into English, it ran as follows:

"You ask, my dear son, whether I have relinquished the great grant made us by Facundo Megares. In effect I have. During the past two years I have twice, acting as governor, conveyed to settlers small tracts from this grant. The conditions under which such a grant must be held are too onerous. Moreover, neither I nor you, nor your son, nor his son will live to see the day when there is not range enough for all the cattle that can be brought into the province. Just now time presses, but in a later letter I shall set forth my reasons in detail."

A second and a third time Dick read the paragraph to make sure that he had not misunderstood it. The meaning was plain. There could be no doubt about it. In black and white he had a statement from old Don Bartolome himself that he considered the grant no longer valid, that he had given it up because he did not think it worth holding. He had but to prove the handwriting in court—a thing easy enough to do, since the Don's bold, stiff writing could be found on a hundred documents—and the Valdes claimants would be thrown out of possession.

Gordon looked in vain for the "later letter" to which Bartolome referred. Either it had never been written or it had been destroyed. But without it he had enough to go on.

Before he left the State House he made a proposal to Miss Underwood to buy the letters from her.

"What do you want with a bunch of old letters?" she asked.

"One of them helps my case. The Don refers to the grant and says he has relinquished his claim."

She nodded at him with brisk approval. "It's fair of you to tell me that." The girl stood for a moment considering, a pencil pressed against her lips. "I suppose the letters are not mine to give. They belong to father. Better see him."

"Where?"

"At the office of the *New Mexican*. Or you can come to the house to-night."

"Believe I'll see him right away."

Within half an hour Dick had bought the bundle of letters for five hundred dollars. He returned to the State House with an order to Kate Underwood to deliver them to him upon demand.

"Dad make a good bargain?" asked Miss Underwood, with a laugh.

Gordon told her the price he had paid.

"If I had telephoned to him what you wanted them for they would have cost you three times as much," she told him, nodding sagely.

"Then I'm glad you didn't. Point of fact you haven't the slightest idea what I want with them."

"To help your suit. Isn't that what you're going to use them for?"

Mildly he answered "Yes," but he did not tell her which suit they were to help.

As he was leaving she spoke to him without looking up from her writing. "Mother and I will be at home this evening, if you'd like to look the house over."

"Thanks. I'd be delighted to come. I'm really awfully interested."

"I see you are," she answered dryly.

Followed by his brown shadows at a respectful distance, Dick walked back to the hotel whistling gaily.

"Some one die and leave you a million dollars, son?" inquired the old miner, with amiable sarcasm.

"Me, I'm just happy because I'm not a Chink," explained his friend, and passed to the hotel writing-room.

He sat down, equipped himself with stationery, and selected a new point for a pen. Half a dozen times he made a start and as often threw a crumpled sheet into the waste-paper basket.

It took him nearly an hour to compose an epistle that suited him. What he had finally to content himself with was as follows:

"DEAR MADAM:—Please find inclosed a bundle of letters that apparently belong to you. They have just come into my possession. I therefore send them to you without delay. Your attention is particularly called to the one marked 'Exhibit A.'"

"Very truly yours, RICHARD MUIR GORDON."

He wrapped up the letters, including his own, sealed the package carefully, and walked downtown to the post office. Here he wrote upon the cover the name and address of Miss Valencia Valdes, then registered the little parcel with a request for a signed receipt after delivery at its destination.

Davis noticed that at dinner his friend was more gay than usual.

"You ce'tainly must have come into that million I mentioned, judging by your actions," he insisted, with a smile.

"Wrong guess, Steve. I've just been giving away a million. That's why I'm hilarious."

"You'll have to give me an easier one, son. Didn't know you had a million."

"Oh, well! A million, or a half, or a quarter, whatever the Moreno claim is worth. I'm not counting nickels. An hour ago I had it in my fist. I've just mailed it, very respectfully yours, to my friend the enemy." "Suppose you talk simple American that your Uncle Steve can understand, boy. What have you been up to?"

Dick told him exultantly.

"But, good Lord, why for did you make such a play? You had 'em where the wool was short. Now you've let loose and you'll have to wait 'steen years while the courts eat up all the profits. Of all the mule-headed chumps—"

"Hold your horses, Steve. I know what I'm doing. Said I was a spy and a thief and a liar, didn't she? Threw the hot shot into me proper for a cheap skate swindler, eh?" The young man laid down his knife, leaned across the table, and wagged a forefinger at Davis. "What do you reckon that young woman is going to think of herself when she opens that registered package and finds the letter that would have put the rollers under her claim *muy pronto?*"

"Think! She'll think you the biggest burro that ever brayed on the San Jacinto range. She'll have a commission appointed to examine you for lunacy. What in Mexico is ailin' you, anyhow? You're sick. That's what's wrong. Love-sick, by Moses!" exploded his friend.

Dick smiled blandly. "You've got another guess coming, Steve. She's going to eat dirt because she misjudged me so. She's going to lie awake nights and figure what play she can make to get even again. Getting hold of those blamed letters is the luckiest shot I've made yet. I was in bad—darned bad. Explanations didn't go. I was just a plain ornery skunk. Then I put over this grand-stand play and change the whole situation. She's the one that's in bad now. Didn't she tell me right off the bat what kind of a hairpin I was? Didn't she drive me off the ranch with that game leg of mine all to the bad? Good enough. Now she finds out I'm a white man she's going to be plumb sore at herself."

"What good does that do you? You're making a fight for the

Rio Chama Valley, ain't you? Or are you just having a kid quarrel with a girl?"

"I wouldn't take the Rio Chama Valley as a gift if I had to steal it from Miss Valdes and her people. Ain't I making enough money up at Cripple Creek for my needs? No, Steve! I'm playing for bigger game than that. Size up my hand beside Don Manuel's, and it looks pretty bum. But I'm going to play it strong. Maybe at the draw I'll fill."

"Mebbe you won't."

"I can bet it like I had an ace full, can't I? Anybody can play poker when he's got a mitt full of big ones. Show me the man that can make two pair back an all-blue hand off the map."

"Go to it, you old sport. My money's on you," grinned the miner admiringly. "I'll go order a wedding present."

Through the pleasant coolness of the evening Dick sauntered along the streets to the Underwood home, nor was his contentment lessened because he knew that at a safe distance the brown shadows still dogged his steps. In a scabbard fitted neatly beneath his left arm rested a good friend that more than once had saved its owner's life. To the fraction of a second Gordon knew just how long it would take him to get this into action in case of need.

Kate Underwood met him at the door and took her guest into the living-room. Beside a student lamp a plump little old lady sat knitting. Somehow even before her soft voice welcomed him the visitor knew that her gentle presence diffused an atmosphere of home.

"Thee is welcome, Mr. Gordon. Kate has been telling us of thee."

The young man gave no evidence of surprise, but Kate explained as a matter of course.

"We are Friends, and at home we still use the old way of address."

"I have very pleasant memories of the Friends. A good old lady who took the place of my own mother was one. It is nice to hear the speech again," answered Gordon.

Presently the conversation drifted to the Valdes family. It appeared that as children Kate and Valencia had known each other. The heiress of the Valdes estates had been sent to Washington to school, and later had attended college in the East. Since her return she had spent most of her time in the valley. So that it happened the two young women had not met for a good many years.

It occurred to Dick that there was a certain aloofness in Miss Underwood's attitude toward Valencia, a reticence that was not quite unfriendliness but retained the right of criticism. She held her judgment as it were in abeyance.

While Miss Underwood was preparing some simple refreshments Gordon learned from her mother that Manuel Pesquiera had been formerly a frequent caller.

"He has been so busy since he moved down to his place on the Rio Chama that we see nothing of him," she explained placidly. "He is a fine type of the best of the old Spanish families. Thee would find him a good friend."

"Or a good foe," the young man added.

She conceded the point with a sigh. "Yes. He is testy. He has the old patrician pride."

After they had eaten cake and ice cream, Kate showed Gordon over the house. It was built of adobe, and the window seats in the thick walls were made comfortable with cushions or filled with potted plants. Navajo rugs and Indian baskets lent the rooms the homey appearance such furnishings always give in the old Southwest. The house was built around a court in the center, fronting on which were long, shaded balconies both on the first and second floor. A profusion of flowering trailers rioted up the pillars and along the upper railing.

"The old families knew how to make themselves comfortable, anyhow," commented the guest.

"Yes, that's the word—comfort. It's not modern or stylish or up to date, but I never saw a house really more comfortable to live in than this," Miss Underwood agreed. She led the way through a French window from the veranda to a large room with a southern exposure. "How do you like this room?"

"Must catch the morning sunshine fine. I like even the old stone fireplace in the corner. Why don't builders nowadays make such rooms?"

"You've saved yourself, Mr. Gordon. This is *the sacred room*. Here the Princess of the Rio Chama was born. This was her room when she was a girl until she went away to school. She slept in that very bed. Down on your knees, sir, and worship at the shrine."

He met with a laugh the cool, light scorn of her banter. Yet something in him warmed to his environment. He had the feeling of having come into more intimate touch with her past than he had yet done. The sight of that plain little bed went to the source of his emotions. How many times had his love knelt beside it in her night-gown and offered up her pure prayers to the God she worshiped!

He made his good-byes soon after their return to Mrs. Underwood. Dick was a long way from a sentimentalist, but he wanted to be alone and adjust his mind to the new conception of his sweetheart brought by her childhood home. It was a night of little moonlight. As he walked toward the hotel he could see nothing of the escort that had been his during the past few days. He wondered if perhaps they had got tired of shadowing his movements.

The road along which he was passing had on both sides of it a row of big cottonwoods, whose branches met in an arch above. Dick, with that instinct for safety which every man-hunter has learned, walked down the middle of the street, eyes and ears alert for the least sign of an ambush.

Two men approached on the plank sidewalk. They were quarreling. Suddenly a knife flashed, and one of the men went with an oath to the ground. Dick reached for his gun and plunged straight for the assailant, who had stooped as if to strike again the prostrate man. The rescuer stumbled over a taut rope and at the same moment a swarm of men fell upon him. Even as he rose and shook off the clutching hands Gordon knew that he was the victim of a ruse.

He had lost his revolver in the fall. With clenched fists he struck hard and sure. They swarmed upon him, so many that they got in each other's way. Now he was down, now up again. They swayed to and fro in a huddle, as does a black bear surrounded by a pack of dogs. Still the man at the heart of the melee struck—and struck—and struck again. Men went down and were trodden under foot, but he reeled on, stumbling as he went, turning, twisting, hitting hard and sure with all the strength that many good clean years in the open had stored within him. Blows fell upon his curly head as it rose now and again out of the storm—blows of guns, of knives, of bony knuckles. Yet he staggered forward, bleeding, exhausted, feeling nothing of the blows, seeing only the distorted faces that snarled on every side of him.

He knew that when he went down it would be to stay. Even as he flung them aside and hammered at the brown faces he felt sure he was lost. The coat was torn from his back. The blood from his bruised and cut face and scalp blinded him. Heavy weights dragged at his arms as they struck wildly and feebly. Iron balls seemed to chain his feet. He plowed doggedly forward, dragging the pack with him. Furiously they beat him, striking themselves as often as they did him. His shoulders began to sway forward. Men leaped upon him from behind. Two he dragged down with him as he went. The sky was blotted out. He was tired—deadly tired. In a great weariness he felt himself sinking together.

The consciousness drained out of him as an ebbing wave does from the sands of the shore.

CHAPTER XIV

MANUEL TO THE RESCUE

Valencia Valdes did not conform closely to the ideal her preceptress at the Washington finishing school had held as to what constitutes a perfect lady. Occasionally her activities shocked Manuel, who held to the ancient view that maidens should come to matrimony with the innocence born of conventual ignorance. He would have preferred his wife to be a clinging vine, but in the case of Valencia this would be impossible.

No woman in New Mexico could ride better than the heiress of the Rio Chama. She could throw a rope as well as some of her *vaqueros*. At least one bearskin lay on the floor of her study as a witness to her prowess as a Diana. Many a time she had fished the river in waders and brought back with her to the ranch a creel full of trout. Years in the untempered sun and wind of the southwest had given her a sturdiness of body unusual in a girl so slenderly fashioned. The responsibility of large affairs had added to this an independence of judgment that would have annoyed Don Manuel if he had been less in love.

Against the advice of both Pesquiera and her foreman she had about a year before this time largely increased her holdings in cattle, at the same time investing heavily in improved breeding stock. Her justification had been that the cost of beef, based on the law of supply and demand, was bound to continue on the rise.

"But how do you know, *Dona*?" her perplexed major domo had asked. "Twenty—fifteen years ago everybody had cattle and lost money. Prices are high to-day, but *manana*—"

"To-morrow they will be higher. It's just a matter of arithmetic, Fernando. There are seventeen million less cattle in the country than there were eight years ago. The government reports say so. Our population is steadily increasing. The people must eat. Since there are fewer cattle they must pay more for their meat. We shall have meat to sell. Is that not simple?"

"*Si, Dona*, but—"

"But in the main we have always been sheep-herders, so we ought always to be? We'll run cattle and sheep, too, Fernando. We'll make this ranch pay as it never has before."

"But the feed—the winter feed, *Senorita*?"

"We'll have to raise our feed. I'm going to send for engineers and find what it will cost to impound, water in the *cordilleras* and run ditches into the valley. We ought to be watering thousands of acres for alfalfa and grain that now are dry."

"It never has been done—not in the time of Don Alvaro or even in that of Don Bartolome."

"And so you think it never can?" she asked, with a smile.

"The Rio Chama Valley is grazing land. It is not for agriculture. Everybody knows that," he insisted doggedly.

"Everybody knows we were given two legs with which to walk, but it is an economy to ride. So we use horses."

Fernando shrugged his shoulders. Of what use to argue with the *dona* when her teeth were set? She was a Valdes, and so would have her way.

That had been a year ago. Now the ditches were built. Fields had been planted to alfalfa and grain. Soon the water would be running through the laterals to irrigate the growing crops. Quietly the young woman at the head of things was revolutionizing the life of the valley by transforming it from a pastoral to a farming community.

This morning, having arranged with the major domo the work of the day, Valencia appeared on the porch dressed for riding. She was going to see the water turned on to the new ditches from the north lateral.

The young mistress of the ranch swung astride the horse that had just been brought from the stables, for she rode man-fashion after the sensible custom of the West. Before riding out of the plaza she stopped to give Pedro some directions about a bunch of yearlings in the corral.

The mailman in charge of the R.F.D. route drove into the yard and handed Valencia a bunch of letters and papers. One of the pieces given her was a rather fat package for which she had to sign a registry receipt.

She handed the mail to Juan and told him to put it on the desk in her office library; then she changed her mind, moved by an impulse of feminine curiosity.

"Give me back that big letter, Juan. I'll just see what it is before I go."

Five minutes later she descended to the porch. "I'm not going riding just now. Keep the horse saddled, Pedro." She had read Dick Gordon's note and the letter marked Exhibit A. Even careless Juan noticed that his mistress was much agitated. Pedro wondered savagely whether that splendid devil *Americano* had done something fresh to annoy the dear saint he worshiped.

Gordon had not overemphasized the effect upon her of his action. Her pride had clung to a belief in his unworthiness as the justification for what she had said and done. Now, with a careless and mocking laugh, he had swept aside all the arguments she had nursed. He had sent to her, so that she might destroy it, the letter that would have put her case out of court. If he had wanted a revenge for her bitter words the American had it now. He had repaid her scorn and contempt with magnanimity. He had heaped coals of fire upon her head, had humiliated her by proving that he was more generous of spirit than she.

Valencia paced the floor of her library in a stress of emotion. It was not her pride alone that had been touched, but the fine instincts of justice and fair play and good will. She had outraged hospitality and sent him packing. She had let him take the long tramp in spite of his bad knee. Her dependents had attempted to murder him. Her best friend had tried to fasten a duel upon him. All over the valley his name had been bandied about as that of one in league with the devil. As an answer to all this outrage that had been heaped upon him he refused to take advantage of this chance-found letter of Bartolome merely because it was her letter and not his. Her heart was bowed down with shame and yet was lifted in a warm glow of appreciation of his quality. Something in her blood sang with gladness. She had known all along that the hateful things she had said to him could not be true. He was her enemy, but—the brave spirit of her went out in a rush to thank God for this proof of his decency.

The girl was all hot for action. She wanted to humble herself in apology. She wanted to show him that she could respond to his generosity. But how? Only one way was open just now.

She sat down and wrote a swift, impulsive letter of contrition. For the wrong she had done him Valencia asked forgiveness. As for the letter he had so generously sent, she must beg him to keep it and use it at the forthcoming trial. It would be impossible for her to accept such a sacrifice of his rights. In the meantime she could assure him that she would always be sorry for the way in which she had misjudged him.

The young woman called for her horse again and rode to Corbett's, which was the nearest post-office. In the envelope with her letter was also the one of her grandfather marked "Exhibit A." She, too, carefully registered the contents before mailing.

As she stood on the porch drawing up her gauntlets a young man cantered into sight. He wore puttees, riding breeches, and a neat corduroy coat. One glance told her it was Manuel. No other rider in the valley had quite the same easy seat in the saddle as the young Spaniard. He drew up sharply in front of Valencia and landed lightly on his feet beside her.

"*Buenos, Senorita.*"

"*Buenos,* cousin." Her shining eyes went eagerly to his. "Manuel, what do you think Mr. Gordon has done?"

He shrugged his shoulders. "How can I guess? That mad American might do anything but show the white feather."

In four sentences she told him.

Manuel clapped his hands in approval. "Bravo! Done like a man. He is at least neither a spy nor a thief."

Valencia smiled with pleasure. Manuel, too, had come out of the test with flying colors. He and Gordon were foes, but he accepted at face value what the latter had done, without any sneers or any sign of jealousy.

"And what shall I do with the letter?" his cousin asked.

"Do with it? Put it in the first fire you see. Shall I lend you a match?"

She shook her head, still with the gleam of a smile on her vivid face. "Too late, Manuel. I have disposed of the dangerous evidence."

"So? Good. You took my advice before I gave it, then."

"Not quite. I couldn't be less generous than our enemy. So I have sent the letter back to him and told him to use it."

The young man gave her his best bow. "Magnificent, but not war. I might have trusted the daughter of Don Alvaro to do a thing so royal. My cousin, I am proud of you."

"What else could I have done and held my self-respect? I had insulted him gratuitously and my people had tried to kill him. The least I could do now was to meet him in a spirit like his own."

"Honors are easy. Let us see what Mr. Gordon will now do."

The sound of a light footfall came to them. A timid voice broke into their conversation.

"May I see *Dona* Valencia—alone—for just a minute?"

Miss Valdes turned. A girl was standing shyly in the doorway. Her soft brown eyes begged pardon for the intrusion.

"You are Juanita, are you not?" the young woman asked.

"*Si, Dona.*"

Pesquiera eliminated himself by going in to get his mail.

"What is it that I can do for you?" asked Valencia.

The Mexican girl broke into an emotional storm. She caught one of her hands in the brown palm of the other with a little gesture of despair.

"They have gone to kill him. Dona. I know it. Something tells me. He will never come back alive." The feeling she had repressed was finding vent in long, irregular sobs.

Valencia felt as if she were being drowned in icy water. The color washed from her cheeks. She had no need to ask who it was that would never come back alive, but she did.

"Who, child? Whom is it that they have gone to kill?"

"The American—*Senor* Gordon."

"Who has gone? And when did they go? Tell me quick."

"Sebastian and Pablo—maybe others—I do not know."

Miss Valdes thought quickly. It might be true. Both the men mentioned had asked for a holiday to go to Santa Fe. What business had they there at this time of the year? Could it be Pablo who had shot at Gordon from ambush? If so, why was he so bitter against the common enemy?

"Juanita, tell me everything. What is it that you know?"

The sobs of the girl increased. She leaned against the door jamb and buried her face in the crook of her arm.

The older girl put an arm around the quivering shoulders and spoke gently. "But listen, child. Tell me all. It may be we can save him yet."

A name came from the muffled lips. It was "Pablo."

Valencia's brain was lit by a flash of understanding. "Pablo is your lover. Is it not so, *nina*?"

The dark crown of soft hair moved up and down in assent. "Oh, *Dona*, he was, but—"

"You have quarreled with him?"

Miss Valdes burned with impatience, but some instinct told her she could not hurry the girl.

"*Si, Senorita*. He quarreled. He said—"

"Yes?"

"—that... that *Senor* Gordon..."

Again, groping for the truth, Valencia found it swiftly.

"You mean that Pablo was jealous?"

"Because I had nursed *Senor* Gordon, because he was kind to me, because—" Juanita had lifted her face to answer. As she spoke the color poured into her cheeks even to her throat, convicting evidence of the cruel embarrassment she felt.

Valencia's hand dropped to her side. When she spoke again the warmth had been banished from her voice. "I see. You nursed Mr. Gordon, did you?"

Juanita's eyes fell before the cold accusation in those of Miss Valdes. "*Si, Senorita.*"

"And he was kind to you? In what way kind?"

The slim Mexican girl, always of the shyest, was bathed in blushes. "He called me... *nina*. He..."

"—made love to you."

A sensation as if the clothes were being torn from her afflicted Juanita. Why did the *Dona* drag her heart out to look at it? Nor did the girl herself know how much or how little Richard Gordon's gay *camaraderie* meant. She was of that type of women who love all that are kind to them. No man had ever been so considerate as this handsome curly-headed American. So dumbly her heart went out to him and made the most of his friendliness. Had he not once put his arm around her shoulder and told her to "buck up" when he came upon her crying because of Pedro? Had he not told her she was the prettiest girl in the neighborhood? And had he not said, too, that she was a little angel for nursing him so patiently?

"*Dona*, I—do—not—know." The words came out as if they were being dragged from her. Poor Juanita would have liked the ground to open up and swallow her.

"Don't you know, you little stupid, that he is playing with you, that he will not marry you?"

"If *Dona* Valencia says so," murmured the Mexican submissively.

"Men are that way, heartless... selfish... vain. But I suppose you led him on," concluded Valencia cruelly.

With a little flare of spirit Juanita looked up. Her courage was for her friend, not for herself.

"*Senor* Gordon is good. He is kind."

"A lot you know about it, child. Have nothing to do with him. His love can only hurt a girl like you. Go back to your Pablo and forget the American. I will see he does not trouble you again."

Juanita began to cry again. She did not want *Senorita* Valdes or anybody else interfering between her and the friend she had nursed. But she knew she could not stop this imperative young woman from doing as she pleased.

"Now tell me how you know that Pablo has gone to injure the American. Did he tell you so?"

"No-o."

"Well, what did he say? What is it that you know?" Valencia's shoe tapped the floor impatiently. "Tell me—tell me!"

"He—Pablo—met me at the corral the day he left. I was in the kitchen and he whistled to me." Juanita gave the information sullenly. Why should *Senorita* Valdes treat her so harshly? She had done no wrong.

"Yes. Go on!"

If she had had the force of character Juanita would have turned on her heel and walked away. But all her life it had been impressed upon her that the will of a Valdes was law to her and her class.

"I do not know... Pablo told me nothing... but he laughed at me, oh, so cruelly! He asked if I... had any messages for my Gringo lover."

"Is that all?"

"All... except that he would show me what happened to foreign devils who stole my love from him. Oh, *Senorita*, do you think he will kill the American?"

Valencia, her white lips pressed tightly together, gave no answer. She was thinking.

"I hate Pablo. He is wicked. I will never speak to him again," moaned Juanita helplessly.

Manuel, coming out of the post-office with his mail, looked at the weeping girl incuriously. It was, he happened to know, a habit of the sex to cry over trifles.

Juanita found in a little nod from Miss Valdes permission to leave. She turned and walked hurriedly away to the adobe cabin where she slept. Before she reached it the walk had become a run.

"Has the young woman lost a ribbon or a lover?" commented Pesquiera, with a smile.

"Manuel, I am worried," answered Valencia irrelevantly.

"What about, my cousin?"

"It's this man Gordon again. Juanita says that Pablo and Sebastian have gone to kill him."

"Gone where?"

"To Santa Fe. They asked for a leave of absence. You know how sullen and suspicious Sebastian is. It is fixed firmly in his head that Mr. Gordon is going to take away his farm."

Manuel's black eyes snapped. He did not propose to let any peons steal from him the punishment he owed this insolent Gordon.

"But Pablo is not a fool. Surely he knows he cannot do such a mad thing."

"Pablo is jealous—and hot-headed." The angry color mounted to the cheeks of the young woman. "He is in love with Juanita and he found out this stranger has been philandering with her. It is abominable. This Gordon has made the silly little fool fall in love with him."

"Oh, if Pablo is jealous—" Pesquiera gave a little shrug of his shoulders. He understood pretty well the temperament of the ignorant Mexican. The young lover was likely to shoot first and think afterward.

Valencia was still thinking of the American. Beneath the olive of her cheeks two angry spots still burned. "I detest that sort of thing. I thought he was a gentleman—and he is only a male flirt... or worse."

"Perhaps—and perhaps not, my cousin. Did Juanita tell you—?"

"She told me enough. All I need to know."

Again the young man's shoulders lifted in a little gesture of humorous resignation. He knew the uncompromising directness of Miss Valdes and the futility of arguing with her. After all, the character of Gordon was none of his business. The man might have made love to Juanita, though he did not look like that kind of a person. In any case the important thing was to save his life.

After a moment's thought he announced a decision. "I shall take the stage for Santa Fe this afternoon. When I have warned the American I'll round up your man-hunters and bring them back to you."

His lady's face thanked him, though her words did not. "You may tell them I said they were to come back at once."

At her cousin's urgent request Miss Valdes stayed to eat luncheon with him at Corbett's, which was a half-way station for the stage and maintained a public eating-house. Even Valencia hesitated a little at this, though she was at heart an emancipated American girl and not a much-chaperoned Spanish maid. But she wanted to repay him for the service he was undertaking so cheerfully, and therefore sacrificed her scruples.

As they were being served by Juanita the stage rolled up and disgorged its passengers. They poured into the dining-room—a mine-owner and his superintendent, a storekeeper from the village at the other end of the valley, a young woman school-teacher from the Indian reservation, a cattleman, and two Mexican sheepmen.

While the fresh horses were being hitched to the stage Pesquiera and his guest stood back a little apart from the others. Corbett brought out a sack containing mail and handed it to the driver. The passengers found again their places.

Pesquiera shook hands with Valencia. His gaze rested for a moment in her dark eyes.

"*Adios, linda*," he said, in a low voice.

The color deepened in her cheeks. She understood that he was telling her how very much he was her lover now and always. "Good-bye, *amigo*," she answered lightly.

Pesquiera took his place on the back seat. The whip of the driver cracked. In a cloud of white dust the stage disappeared around a bend in the road.

Valencia ordered her horse brought, and left for the ranch. Having dispatched Manuel to the scene of action, it might be supposed that she would have awaited the issue without farther activity. But on the way home she began to reflect that her cousin would not reach Santa Fe until next morning, and there was always a chance that this would be too late. As soon as she reached the ranch she called up the station where the stage connected with the train. To the operator she dictated a message to be wired to Richard Gordon. The body of it ran thus:

"Have heard that attack may be made upon your life. Please do not go out alone or at night at all. Answer."

She gave urgent instructions that if necessary to reach Gordon her telegram be sent to every hotel in the city and to his lawyer, Thomas M. Fitt.

Now that she had done all she could the young woman tried to put the matter out of her mind by busying herself with the affairs of the ranch. She had a talk with a cattle buyer, after which she rode out to see the engineer who had charge of the building of the irrigation system she had installed. An answer would, she was sure, be awaiting her upon her return home.

Her anticipation was well founded. One of the housemaids told her that the operator at San Jacinto had twice tried to get her on the telephone. The mistress of the ranch stepped at once to the receiver.

"Give me San Jacinto," she said to the operator.

As soon as she was on the wire with the operator he delivered the message he had for her. It was from Santa Fe and carried the signature of Stephen Davis:

"Gordon has been missing since last night. I fear the worst. For God's sake, tell me what you know."

Valencia leaned against the telephone receiver and steadied herself. She felt strangely faint. The wall opposite danced up and down and the floor swayed like the deck of a vessel in a heavy sea. She set her teeth hard to get a grip on herself. Presently the wave of light-headedness passed.

She moved across the room and sank down into a chair in front of her desk. They had then murdered him after all. She and her people were responsible for his death. There was nothing to be done now—nothing at all.

Then, out of the silence, a voice seemed to call to her—the voice of Richard Gordon, faint and low, but clear. She started to her feet and listened, shaken to the soul by this strange summons from that world which lay beyond the reach of her physical senses. What could it mean? She had the body of a healthy young animal. Her nerves never played her any tricks. But surely there had come to her a call for help not born of her own excited fancy.

In an instant she had made up her mind. Her finger pressed an electric button beside the desk, and almost simultaneously a second one. The maid who appeared in the doorway in answer to the first ring found her mistress busily writing.

Valencia looked up. "Rosario, pack a suitcase for me with clothes for a week. Put in my light brown dress and a couple of shirt-waists. I'll be up presently." Her gaze passed to the major domo who now stood beside the maid. "I'm going to Santa Fe to-night, Fernando. Order the grays to be hitched to the buggy."

"To-night! But, *Senorita*, the train has gone."

"Juan will go with me. We'll drive right through. My business is important."

"But it is seventy miles to Santa Fe, and part of the way over mountain roads," he protested.

"Yes. We should reach there by morning. I mean to travel all night. Make the arrangements, please, and tell Juan. Then return here. I want to talk over with you the ranch affairs. You will have charge of the ditches, too, during my absence. Don't argue, Fernando, but do as I say."

The old man had opened his mouth to object, but he closed it without voicing his views. A little smile, born of his pride in her wilfulness, touched his lips and wrinkled the parchment skin. Was she not a Valdes? He had served her father and her grandfather. To him, therefore, she could do no wrong.

CHAPTER XV

ONE THOUSAND DOLLARS REWARD

The night of his disappearance Dick had sauntered forth from the hotel with the jaunty assurance to Davis that he was going to call on a young lady. He offered no further details, and his friend asked for none, though he wondered a little what young woman in Santa Fe had induced Gordon to change his habits. The old miner had known him from boyhood. His partner had never found much time for the society of eligible maidens. He had been too busy living to find tea-cup discussions about life interesting. The call of adventure had absorbed his youth, and he had given his few mature years ardently to the great American game of money-making. It was not that he loved gold. What Richard Gordon cared for was the battle, the struggle against both honorable and unscrupulous foe-men for success. He fought in the business world only because it was the test of strength. Money meant power. So he had made money.

It was not until Dick failed to appear for breakfast next morning that Davis began to get uneasy. He sent a bellboy to awaken Gordon, and presently the lad came back with word that he could get no answer to his knocks. Instantly Steve pushed back his chair and walked out of the room to the desk in the lobby.

"Got a skeleton key to Mr. Gordon's room—317, I think it is?" he demanded.

"Yes. We keep duplicate keys. You see, Mr. Davis, guests go away and carry the keys—"

"Then I want it. Afraid something's wrong with my friend. He's always up early and on hand for breakfast. He hasn't showed up this mo'ning. The bell hop can't waken him. I tell you something's wrong."

"Oh, I reckon he'll turn up all right." The clerk turned to the key rack. "Here's the key to Room 317. Mr. Gordon must have left it here. Likely he's gone for a walk."

Davis shook his head obstinately. "Don't believe it. I'm going up to see, anyhow."

Within five minutes he discovered that the bed in Room 317 had not been slept in the previous night. He was thoroughly alarmed. Gordon had no friends in the town likely to put him up for the night. Nor was he the sort of rounder to dissipate his energies in all-night debauchery. Dick had come to Santa Fe for a definite purpose. The old miner knew from long experience that he would not be diverted from it for the sake of the futile foolish diversions known by some as pleasure. Therefore the mind of Davis jumped at once to the conclusion of foul play.

And if foul play, then the Valdes claimants to the Rio Chamo Valley were the guilty parties. He blamed himself bitterly for having let Dick venture out alone, for having taken no precautions whatever to guard him against the Mexicans who had already once attempted his life.

"I'm a fine friend. Didn't even find out who he was going out to call on. Fact is, I didn't figure he was in any danger so long as he was in town here," he explained to the sheriff.

He learned nothing either at the police headquarters or at the newspaper offices that threw light on the disappearance of Gordon. No murder had been reported during the night. No unusual disturbance of any kind had occurred, so far as could be learned.

Before noon he had the town plastered with posters in English and in Spanish offering a reward of five hundred dollars for news leading to the recovery of Richard Gordon or for evidence leading to the conviction of his murderers in case he was dead. This brought two callers to the hotel almost at once. One was the attorney Fitt, the other a young woman who gave her name as Kate Underwood. Fitt used an hour of the old miner's time to no purpose, but the young woman brought with her one piece of news.

"I want to know when Mr. Gordon was last seen," she explained, "because he was calling on my mother and me last night and left about ten o'clock."

The little man got to his feet in great excitement. "My dear young woman, you're the very person I've been wanting to see. He told me he was going calling, but I'm such a darned chump I didn't think to ask where. Is Dick a friend of your family?"

"No, hardly that. I met him when he came to our office in the State House to look up the land grant papers. We became friendly and I asked him to call because we own the old Valdes house, and I thought he would like to see it." She added, rather dryly: "You haven't answered my question."

"I'll say that so far as I know you are the last person who

ever saw Dick alive except his murderers," Davis replied, a gleam of tears in his eyes.

"Oh, it can't be as bad as that," she cried. "They wouldn't go that far."

"Wouldn't they? He was shot at from ambush while we were out riding one day in the Chama Valley."

"By whom?"

"By a young Mexican—one of Miss Valdes servants."

"You don't mean that Valencia—?"

She stopped, unwilling to put her horrified thought into words. He answered her meaning.

"No, I reckon not. She wanted Dick to tell her who it was, so she could punish the man. But that doesn't alter the facts any. He was shot at. That time the murderer missed, but maybe this time—"

Miss Underwood broke in sharply. "Do you know that he has been followed ever since he came to town, that men have dogged his steps everywhere?"

Davis leaned across the table where he was sitting. "How do you know?" he questioned eagerly.

"I saw them and warned him. He laughed about it and said he knew already. He didn't seem at all worried."

"Worried! He's just kid enough to be tickled to death about it," snapped the miner, masking his anxiety with irritation. "He hadn't sense enough to tell me for fear it would disturb me—and I hadn't the sense to find out in several days what you did in five minutes."

Davis and Miss Underwood went together over every foot of the road between her home and the hotel. One ray of hope they got from their examination of the ground he must have traversed to reach the El Tovar, as the hotel was named. At one spot—where a double row of cottonwoods lined the road—a fence had been knocked down and many feet had trampled the sandy pasture within. Steve picked up a torn piece of cloth about six inches by twelve in dimension. It had evidently been a part of a coat sleeve. He recognized the pattern as that of the suit his friend had been wearing.

"A part of his coat all right," he said. "They must have bushwhacked him here. By the foot-prints there were a good many of them."

"I'm glad there were."

"Why?"

"For two reasons," the girl explained. "In the first place, if they had wanted to kill him, one or two would have been enough. They wouldn't take any more than was necessary into their confidence."

"That's right. Your head's level there."

"And, in the second place, two men can keep a secret, but six or eight can't. Some one of them is bound to talk to his sweetheart or wife or friend."

"True enough. That five hundred dollars might get one of 'em, too."

"Somehow I believe he is alive. His enemies have taken him away somewhere—probably up into the hills."

"But why?"

"You ought to know that better than I do. What could they gain by it?"

He scratched his gray head. "Search me. They couldn't aim to hold him till after the trial. That would be a kid's play."

"Couldn't they get him to sign some paper—something saying that he would give up his claim—or that he would sell out cheap?"

"No, they couldn't," the old man answered grimly. "But they might think they could. I expect that's the play. Dick never in the world would come through, though. He's game, that boy is. The point is, what will they do when they find he stands the acid?"

Miss Underwood looked quickly at him, then looked quickly away. She knew what they would do. So did Davis.

"No, that's not the point. We must find him—just as soon as we can. Stir this whole town up and rake it with a fine-tooth comb. See if any of Miss Valdes' peons are in town. If they are have them shadowed."

They separated presently, she to go to the State House, he to return to the El Tovar. There he found the telegram from Miss Valdes awaiting him. Immediately he dictated an answer.

Before nightfall a second supply of posters decorated walls and billboards. The reward was raised to one thousand dollars for information that would lead to the finding of Richard Gordon alive and the same sum for evidence sufficient to convict his murderers in case he was dead. It seemed impossible that in so small a place, with everybody discussing the mysterious disappearance, the affair could long remain a secret. Davis did not doubt that Miss Underwood was correct in her assumption that the assailants of Gordon had carried him with them into some hidden pocket of the hills, in which case it might take longer to run them to earth. The great danger that he feared was panic on the part of the abductors. To cover their tracks they might kill him and leave this part of the country. The closer pursuit pressed on them the more likely this was to happen. It behooved him to move with the greatest care.

CHAPTER XVI

VALENCIA MAKES A PROMISE

When Manuel descended from the El Tovar hack which had brought him from the station to that hotel the first person he saw standing upon the porch was Valencia Valdes. He could hardly believe his eyes, for of course she could not be here. He had left her at Corbett's, had taken the stage and the train, and now found her waiting for him. The thing was manifestly impossible. Yet here she was.

Swiftly she came down the steps to meet him.

"Manuel, we are too late. Mr. Gordon has gone."

"Gone where?" he asked, his mind dazed as it moved from one puzzle to another.

"We don't know. He was attacked night before last and carried away, whether dead or alive we have no proof."

"One thing at a time, Valencia. How did you get here?"

"I drove across the mountains—started when I got the news from Mr. Davis that his friend had disappeared."

"Do you mean that you drove all night—along mountain roads?" he asked, amazed.

"Of course. I had to get here." She dismissed this as a trifle with a little gesture of her hand. "Manuel, we must find him. I believe he is alive. This is some of Pablo's work. Down in old-town some one must know where he is. Bring him to me and I'll make him tell what he has done with Mr. Gordon."

Pesquiera was healthily hungry. He would have liked to sit down to a good breakfast, but he saw that his cousin was laboring under a heavy nervous tension. Cheerfully he gave up his breakfast for the present.

But when, three hours later, he returned from the old adobe Mexican quarter Manuel had nothing to report but failure. Pablo had been seen by several people, but not within the past twenty-four hours. Nor had anything been seen of Sebastian. The two men had disappeared from sight as completely as had Gordon.

Valencia, in the privacy of one of the hotel parlors, broke down and wept for the first time. Manuel tried to comfort her by taking the girl in his arms and petting her. She submitted to his embrace, burying her face in his shoulder.

"Oh, Manuel, I'm a—a murderess," she sobbed.

"You're a goose," he corrected. "Haven't you from the first tried to save this man from his own rashness? You're not to blame in any way, Val."

"Yes... Yes," she sobbed. "Pablo and Sebastian would never have dared touch him if they hadn't known that I'd quarreled with him. It all comes back to that."

"That's pure nonsense. For that matter, I don't believe he's dead at all. We'll find him, as gay and insolent as ever, I promise you."

Hope was buoyant in the young man's heart. For the first time he held his sweetheart in his arms. She clung to him, as a woman ought to her lover, palpitant, warm, and helpless. Of course they would find this pestiferous American who had caused her so much worry. And then he—Manuel— would claim his reward.

"Do you think so... really? You're not just saying so because...?" Her olive cheek turned the least in the world toward him.

Manuel trod on air. He felt that he could have flown across the range on the wings of his joy.

"I feel sure of it, *nina*." Daring much, his hand caressed gently the waves of heavy black hair that brushed his cheek.

Almost in a murmur she answered him. "Manuel, find him and save him. Afterward..."

"Afterward, *alma mia?*"

She nodded. "I'll... do what you ask."

"You will marry me?" he cried, afraid to believe that his happiness had come at last.

"Yes."

"Valencia, you love me?"

She trod down any doubts she might feel. Was he not the one

suitable mate for her of all the men she knew?

"How can I help it. You are good. You are generous. You serve me truly." Gently she disengaged herself and wiped her eyes with a lace kerchief. "But we must first find the American."

"I'll find him. Dead or alive I'll bring him to you. Dear heart, you've given me the strength that moves mountains."

A little smile fought for life upon her sad face. "You'll not have strength unless you eat. Poor Manuel, I think you lost your breakfast. I ordered luncheon to be ready for us early. We'll eat now."

A remark of Manuel during luncheon gave his vis-a-vis an idea.

"Mr. Davis is most certainly thorough. I never saw a town so plastered with bills before," he remarked.

Valencia laid down her knife and fork as she looked at him. "Let's offer a reward for Pablo and Sebastian—say, a hundred dollars. That would bring us news of them."

"You're right," he agreed. "I'll get bills out this afternoon. Perhaps I'd better say no incriminating questions will be asked of those giving us information."

Stirred to activity by the promise of such large rewards, not only the sheriff's office and the police, but also private parties scoured the neighboring country for traces of the missing man or his captors. Every available horse in town was called into service for the man-hunt. Others became sleuths on foot and searched cellars and empty houses for the body of the man supposed to have been murdered. Never in its history had so much suspicion among neighbors developed in the old-town. Many who could not possibly be connected with the crime were watched jealously lest they snap up one of the rewards by stumbling upon evidence that had been overlooked.

False clews in abundance were brought to Davis and Pesquiera. Good citizens came in with theories that lacked entirely the backing of any evidence. One of these was that a flying machine had descended in the darkness and that Gordon had been carried away by a friend to avoid the payment of debts he was alleged to owe. The author of this explanation was a stout old lady of militant appearance who carried a cotton umbrella large enough to cover a family. She was extraordinarily persistent and left in great indignation to see a lawyer because Davis would not pay her the reward.

That day and the next passed with the mystery still unsolved. Valencia continued to stay at the hotel instead of opening the family town house, probably because she had brought no servants with her from the valley and did not know how long she would remain in the city. She and Manuel called upon the Underwoods to hear Kate's story, but from it they gathered nothing new. Mrs. Underwood welcomed them with the gentle kindness that characterized her, but Kate was formal and distant.

"She doesn't like me," Valencia told her cousin as soon as they had left. "I wonder why. We were good enough friends as children."

Manuel said nothing. He stroked his little black mustache with the foreign manner he had inherited. If he had cared to do so perhaps he could have explained Kate Underwood's stiffness. Partly it was embarrassment and partly shyness. He knew that there had been a time—before Valencia's return from college—when Kate lacked very little of being in love with him. He had but to say the word to have become engaged—and he had not said it. For, while on a visit to the East, he had called upon his beautiful cousin and she had won his love at once. This had nipped in the bud any embryonic romance that might otherwise have been possible with Kate.

A little old Mexican woman with a face like wrinkled leather was waiting to see them in front of the hotel.

"*Senor* Pesquiera?" she asked, with a little bob of the body meant to be a bow.

"Yes."

"And *Senorita* Valdes?"

"That is my name," answered Valencia.

"Will the *senor* and the *senorita* take a walk? The night is fine."

"Where?" demanded Manuel curtly.

"Into old-town, *senor*."

"You have something to tell us."

"To show you, *senor*—for a hundred dollars."

"Sebastian—or is it Pablo?" cried Valencia, in a low voice.

"I say nothing, *senorita*" whined the old woman. "I show you; then you pay. Is it not so?"

"Get the money, Manuel," his cousin ordered quietly.

Manuel got it from the hotel safe. He took time also to get from his room a revolver. Gordon had fallen victim to an ambush and he did not intend to do so if he could help it. In his own mind he had no doubt that some of their countrymen were selling either Pablo or Sebastian for the reward, but it was better to be safe than to be sorry.

The old crone led them by side streets into the narrow adobe-lined roads of old-town. They passed through winding alleys and between buildings crumbling with age. Always Manuel watched, his right hand in his coat pocket. At the entrance to a little court a man emerged from the shadow of a wall. He whispered with the old dame for a minute.

"Come. Make an end of this and show us what you have to show, *muy pronto*," interrupted Manuel impatiently.

"In good time, *senor*," the man apologized.

"Just a word first, my friend. I have a revolver in my hand. If there is trickery in your mind, better give it up. I'm a dead shot, and I'll put the first bullet through your heart. Now lead on."

The Mexican threw up his hands in protest to all the saints that his purpose was good. He would assuredly keep faith, *senor*.

"See you do," replied the Spaniard curtly.

Their guide rapped three times on a door of a tumble-down shack. Cautiously it was opened a few inches. There was another whispered conversation.

"The *senor* and the *senorita* can come in," said the first man, standing aside.

Manuel restrained the young woman by stretching his left arm in front of her.

"Just a moment. Light a lamp, my friends. We do not go forward in the dark."

At this there was a further demur, but finally a match flickered and a lamp was lit. Manuel moved slowly forward into the room, followed by Valencia. In a corner of the room a man lay bound upon the floor, his back toward them. One of the men rolled him over as if he had been a sack of potatoes. The face into which they looked had been mauled and battered, but Valencia had no trouble in recognizing it.

"Sebastian!" she cried.

He said nothing. A sullen, dogged look rested on his face. Manuel had seen it before on the countenance of many men. He knew that the sheep grazer could not be driven to talk.

Miss Valdes might have known it, too, but she was too impatient for finesse. "What have you done with Mr. Gordon? Tell me—now—at once," she commanded.

The man's eyes did not lift to meet hers. Nor did he answer a single word.

"First, our hundred dollars, *Senorita*," one of the men reminded her.

"It will be paid when you deliver Sebastian to us in the street with his hands tied behind him," Manuel promised.

They protested, grumbling that they had risked enough already when they had captured him an hour earlier. But in the end they came to Pesquiera's condition. The prisoner's hands were tied behind him and his feet released so that he could walk. Manuel slid one arm under the right one of Sebastian. The fingers of his left hand rested on the handle of a revolver in his coat pocket.

Valencia, all impatience, could hardly restrain herself until they were alone with their prisoner. She walked on the other side of her cousin, but as soon as they reached the Plaza she stopped.

"Where is he, Sebastian? What have you done with him? I warn you it is better to tell all you know," she cried sternly.

He looked up at her doggedly, moistened his lips, and looked down again without a word.

"Speak!" she urged imperiously. "Where is Mr. Gordon? Tell me he is alive. And what of Pablo?"

Manuel spoke in a low voice. "My cousin, you are driving him to silence. Leave him to me. He must be led, not driven."

Valencia was beyond reason. She felt that every minute lost was of tremendous importance. If Gordon was alive they must get help to him at once. All her life she had known Sebastian. When she had been a little tot he had taught her how to ride and how to fish. Since her return from college she had renewed acquaintance with him. Had she not been good to his children when they had small-pox? Had she not sold him his place cheaper than any other man could have bought it? Why, then, should he assume she was his enemy? Why should he distrust her? Why, above all, had he done this foolish and criminal thing?

Her anger blazed as she recalled all this and more. She would show Sebastian that because she had been indulgent he could not trade defiantly upon her kindness.

"No," she told Manuel. "No. I shall deal with him myself. He will speak or I shall turn him over to the sheriff."

"Let us at least go to the hotel, Valencia. We do not want to gather a crowd on the street."

"As you please."

They reached the hotel parlor and Valencia gave Sebastian one more chance.

The man shuffled uneasily on his feet, but did not answer.

"Very well," continued Miss Valdes stiffly, "it is not my fault that you will have to go to the penitentiary and leave your children without support."

Manuel tried to stop her, but Valencia brushed past and left the room. She went straight to a telephone and was connected with the office of the sheriff. After asking that an officer be sent at once to arrest a man whom she was holding as prisoner, she hung up the receiver and returned to the parlor.

In all she could not have been absent more than five minutes, but when she reached the parlor it was empty. Both Manuel and his prisoner had gone.

CHAPTER XVII

AN OBSTINATE MAN

When Richard Gordon came back from unconsciousness to a world of haziness and headaches he was quite at a loss to account for his situation. He knew vaguely that he was lying flat on his back and that he was being jolted uncomfortably to and fro. His dazed brain registered sensations of pain both dull and sharp from a score of bruised nerve centers. For some reason he could neither move his hands nor lift his head. His body had been so badly jarred by the hail of blows through which he had plowed that at first his mind was too blank to give him explanations.

Gradually he recalled that he had been in a fight. He remembered a sea of faces, the thud of fists, the flash of knives. This must be the reason why every bone ached, why the flesh on his face was caked and warm moisture dripped from cuts in his scalp. It dawned upon him that he could not move his arms because they were tied and that the interference with his breathing was caused by a gag. When he opened his eyes he saw nothing, but whenever his face or hands stirred from the jolting something light and rough brushed his flesh; An odor of alfalfa filled his nostrils. He guessed that he was in a wagon and covered with hay.

Where were they taking him? Why had they not killed him at once? Who was at the bottom of the attack upon him? Already his mind was busy with the problem.

Presently the jolting ceased. He could hear guarded voices. The alfalfa was thrown aside and he was dragged from his place and carried down some steps. The men went stumbling through the dark, turning first to the right, and then to the left. They groped their way into a room and dropped him upon a bed. Even now they struck no light, but through a small window near the ceiling moonbeams entered and relieved somewhat the inky blackness.

"Is he dead?" someone asked in Spanish.

"No. His eyes were open as we brought him in," answered a second voice guardedly.

They stood beside the bed and looked down at their prisoner. His eyes were getting accustomed to the darkness. He saw that one of the men was Pablo Menendez. The other, an older Mexican with short whiskers, was unknown to him.

"He fought like a devil from hell. Roderigo's arm is broken. Not one of us but is marked," said the older man admiringly.

"My head is ringing yet, Sebastian," agreed Pablo. "*Dios*, how he slammed poor Jose down. The blood poured from his nose and mouth. Never yet have I seen a man fight so fierce and so hard as this *Americano*. He may be the devil himself, but his claws are clipped now. And here he lies till he does as we want, or—" The young Mexican did not finish his sentence, but the gleam in his eyes was significant.

Pablo stooped till his eyes were close to those of the bound man. "*Senor,* shall I take the gag from your mouth? Will you swear not to cry out and not to make any noise?"

Gordon nodded.

"So, but if you do the road to Paradise will be short and swift," continued Menendez. "Before your shout has died away you will be dead. *Sabe, Senor?*"

He unknotted the towel at the back of his prisoner's head and drew it from Dick's mouth. Gordon expanded his lungs in a deep breath before he spoke coolly to his gaoler.

"Thank you, Menendez. You needn't keep your fist on that gat. I've no intention of committing suicide until after I see you hanged."

"Which will be never, *Senor* Gordon," replied Pablo rapidly in Spanish. "You will never leave here alive except on terms laid down by us."

"Interesting if true—but not true, I think," commented Dick pleasantly. "You have made a mistake, my friends, and you will have to pay for it."

"If we have made a mistake it can yet be remedied, *Senor*" retorted Pablo quietly. "We have but to make an end of you and behold! all is well again."

"Afraid not, my enthusiastic young friend. Too many in the secret. Someone will squeal, and the rest of you— particularly you two ringleaders—will be hanged by the neck. It takes only ordinary intelligence to know that. Therefore I am quite safe, even though I have a confounded headache and a rising fever." Gordon added with cheerful solicitude: "I do hope I'm not going to get sick on your hands. It's rather a habit of mine, you know. But, really, you can't blame me this time."

A danger signal flared in the eyes of the young Mexican. "Better not, *Senor*. You will here have no young and charming nurse to wait upon you."

"Meaning Mrs. Corbett?" asked the prisoner, smiling up impudently.

"Whose heart your soft words can steal away from him to whom it belongs," continued Pablo furiously.

"Sho, I reckon Corbett—"

"*Mil diablos!*"

A devil of jealousy was burning out of the black eyes that blazed into those of the American. It was no longer possible for Dick to miss the menace and its meaning. The Mexican was speaking of Juanita. He believed that his prisoner had been making love to the girl and his heart was black with hate because of it.

Gordon looked at him steadily, then summed up with three derisive words. "You damn fool!"

Something in the way he said them shook Pablo's conviction. Was it possible after all that his jealousy had been useless? Juanita had told him that all through his delirium this man had raved of Miss Valdes. Perhaps—But, no, had he not with his own eyes seen the man bantering Juanita while the color came and went in her wild rose cheeks? Had he not seen him lean on her shoulder as he hobbled out to the porch, just as a lover might on that of his sweetheart?

With an oath Pablo turned sullenly away. He knew he was

no match for this man at any point. Yet he was a leader among his own people because of the force in him.

Gordon slept little during the night. He had been so badly beaten that outraged nature took her revenge in a feverish restlessness that precluded any real rest. With the coming of day the temperature subsided. Pablo brought a basin of water and a sponge, with which he washed the bloody face and head of the bound man.

Dick observed that his nurse had a few marks of his own as souvenirs of the battle. The cheek bone had been laid open by a blow that must have been made with his knuckles. One eye was half shut, and beneath it was a deep purple swelling.

"Had quite a little jamboree, didn't we?" remarked Gordon, with a grin. "I'll bet you lads mussed my hair up some."

Pablo said nothing, but after he had made his unwilling guest as presentable and comfortable as possible he proceeded to business.

"You want to know why we have made you prisoner, *Senor* Gordon?" he suggested. "It has perhaps occur to you that it would have been much easier to shoot you and be done?"

"Yes, that has struck me, Menendez. I reckon your nerve didn't quite run to murder maybe."

"Not so. I spare you because you save my brother's life after he shoot at you. But I exact conditions. So?"

The eyes of the miner had grown hard and steelly. The lids had closed on them so that only slits were open. "Let's hear them."

"First, that you give what is called word of honor not to push any charges against those taking you prisoner."

"Pass that for the present," ordered Dick curtly. "Number two please."

"That you sign a paper drawn up by a lawyer giving all your rights in the Rio Chama Valley to Senorita Valdes and promise never to go near the valley again."

"Nothing doing," answered the prisoner promptly, his jaws snapping tight.

"But yes—most assuredly yes. I risk much to save your life. But you must go to meet me, *Senor*. Is a man's life not worth all to him? So? Sign, and you live."

The eyes of the men had fastened—the fierce, black, eager ones of the Mexican and the steelly gray ones of the Anglo-Saxon. There was the rigor of battle in that gaze, the grinding of rapier on rapier. Gordon was a prisoner in the hands of his enemy. He lay exhausted from a terrible beating. That issues of life and death hung in the balance a child might have guessed. But victory lay with the white man. The lids of Menendez fell over sullen, angry eyes.

"You are a fool, *Senor*. We go to prison for no man who is our enemy. Pouf! When the hour comes I snuff out your life like that." And Pablo snapped his fingers airily.

"Maybe—and maybe not. I figure on living to be an old man. Tell you what I'll do, Menendez. Turn me loose and I'll forget about our little rumpus last night. I'd ought to send you to the pen, but I'll consent to forego that pleasure."

Sulkily Pablo turned away. What could one do with a

madman who insisted on throwing his life away? The young Mexican was not a savage, though the barbaric strain in his wild lawless blood was still strong. He did not relish the business of killing in cold blood even the man he hated.

"If you kill me you'll hang," went on Gordon composedly. "You'll never get away with it. Your own friends will swear your neck into a noose. Your partner Sebastian—you'll excuse me if I appear familiar, but I don't know the gentleman's other name—will turn State's evidence to try to save his own neck. But I reckon he'll have to climb the ladder, too."

Sebastian pushed aside his companion angrily and took the American by the throat.

"*Por Dios*, I show you. If I hang I hang—but you—" His muscular fingers tightened till the face of his enemy grew black. But the eyes—the steady, cool, contemptuous eyes—still looked into his defiantly.

Pablo dragged his accomplice from the bedside. The time might come for this, but it was not yet.

It had been a close thing for Gordon. If those lean, strong fingers had been given a few seconds more at his throat they would have snapped the cord of life. But gradually the distorted face resumed its natural hue as the coughing, strangling man began to breathe again.

"Your—friend—is—impetuous," Dick suggested to Pablo as soon as he could get the words out one at a time.

"He will shake the life out of you as a terrier does that of a rat," Pablo promised vindictively.

"There's no fun—in being strangled, as you'll both—find out later," the prisoner retorted whimsically but with undaunted spirit.

Sebastian had left the room. At the expiration of half an hour he returned with a tray, upon which were two plates with food and two cups of steaming coffee. The Mexicans ate their ham and their *frijoles* and drank their coffee. The prisoner they ignored.

"Don't I draw even a Libby Prison allowance?" the American wanted to know.

"You eat and you drink after you have signed the paper," Pablo told him.

"I always did think we ate too much and too often. Much obliged for a chance to work out my theories."

Gordon turned his back upon them, his face to the wall. Presently, in spite of the cramped position necessitated by his bound arms, he yielded to weariness and fell asleep. Sebastian lay down in a corner of the room and also slept. He and Pablo would have to relieve each other as watchmen so long as they held their prisoner. For that reason they must get what rest they could during the day.

Menendez found himself the victim of conflicting emotions. It had been easy while they were plotting the abduction to persuade himself that the man would grant anything to save his life. Now he doubted this. Looking clown at the battered face of the miner, so lean and strong and virile, he could not withhold a secret reluctant admiration. How was it possible for him to sleep so easily and lightly while he lay within the shadow of violent death? There was even a little smile about the corners of his mouth, as if he were enjoying pleasant dreams. Never had Pablo known another man like this one. Had he not broken the spirit of that outlaw devil Teddy in ten minutes? Who else could shoot the heads off chickens at a distance as he had done? Was there another in New Mexico that could, though taken at advantage, put up so fierce a fight against big odds? The young Mexican hated him because of Juanita and his opposition to Miss Valdes. But the untamed and gallant spirit of the young man went out in spite of himself in homage to the splendid courage and efficiency of his victim.

Not till the middle of the afternoon did Gordon awaken. He was surprised to find that his hands were free. Of Menendez he asked an explanation.

Pablo gave him none. How could he say that he was ashamed to keep him tied while two armed men were in the room to watch him?

"Move from that bed and I'll blow your brains out," the Mexican growled in Spanish.

Presently Pablo brought him a tin dipper filled with water.

"Drink, *Senor*" he ordered ungraciously.

Dick drank the last drop and smiled at his guard gratefully. "You're white in spots, Mr. Miscreant, though you hate to think it of yourself," he said lightly.

Odd as it may seem, Gordon found a curious pleasure in exploring the mind of the young man. He detected the struggle going on in it, and he made remarks so uncannily wise that the Mexican was startled at his divination. The miner held no grudge. These men were his enemies because they thought him a selfish villain who ought to be frustrated in his designs. Long ago, in that school of experience which had made him the hard, competent man he was, Dick had learned the truth of the saying that to know all is to forgive all. He himself had done bold and lawless things often enough, but it was seldom that he did a mean one. Warily alert though he was for a chance to escape, his feelings were quite impersonal toward these Mexicans. Confronted with the need, he would kill if he must to save himself; but it would not be because he was vindictive.

Dick's mind was alert to every chance of escape. He studied his situation as well as he could without moving from the bed. From the glimpse of the house he had had as the two men carried him in he knew that it was a large, modern one set in grounds of considerable size. He had been brought down a flight of steps and was now in the basement. Was the house an unoccupied one? Or was it in the possession of some one friendly to the scheme upon which the Mexicans had engaged?

A suspicion had startled him just after the men finished eating, but he had dismissed it as a fantasy of his excited imagination. Sebastian, carrying out the dishes, had dropped a spoon and left it lying beside the bed. Dick contrived, after he had wakened, to roll close to the edge and look down. The spoon was still there. Two letters were engraved upon the handle. They were A.V. If these stood for Alvaro Valdes, then this must be the town house of Valencia, and she was probably a party to his abduction.

He could not without distress of heart accept such a conclusion. She was his enemy, but she had seemed to him so frank and generous a one that complicity in a plot of this nature had no part in the picture of her his mind had drawn. He wrestled with the thought of this until he could stand it no longer.

"Did Miss Valdes come to town herself, or is she letting you run this abduction, Menendez?" he asked suddenly.

Pablo repeated stupidly, "Miss Valdes—the *senorita*?"

The keen, hard eyes of Gordon did not lift for an instant from those of the other man. "That's what I said."

It occurred to the Mexican that this was a chance to do a stroke of business for his mistress. He would show the confident *Americano* what place he held in her regard.

His shoulders lifted in a shrug. "You are clevair, *Senor*. How do you know the *senorita* knows?"

"This is her house. She told you to bring me here."

Pablo was surprised. "So? You know it is her house?"

"Surest thing you know."

"The *senorita* trusts me. She is at the ranch."

"But you are acting under her orders?"

"If the *senor* pleases."

Dick turned his back to the wall again. His heart was bitter within him. He had thought her a sportsman, every inch a thoroughbred. But she had set her peons to spy on him and to attack him—ten to one in their favor—so that she might force him to sign away his rights to her. Very well. He would show her whether she could drive him to surrender, whether she could starve him into doing what he did not want to do.

The younger Mexican wakened Sebastian late in the

afternoon and left him to guard the prisoner while he went into the town to hear what rumors were flying about the affair. About an hour later he returned, bringing with him some provisions, a newspaper, and a handbill. The latter he tossed to Gordon.

"Senor, I never saw five hundred dollars dangling within reach before. Shall I go to your friend and give him information?" asked Pablo.

Dick read the poster through with interest. "Good old Steve. He's getting busy. Inside of twenty-four hours he'll ferret out this spot."

"It may be too late," Pablo flung back significantly. "If they press us hard we'll finish the job and make a run for it."

They were talking in Spanish, as they did most of the time. The prisoner read aloud the offer on the handbill.

"Please notice that I'm worth no more alive than you are if I'm dead. I reckon this town is full of friends of yours anxious to earn five hundred plunks by giving a little information. Let me ask a question of you. Suppose you do finish the job and hit the trail. Where would you go?"

"The hills are full of pockets. We could hide and watch a chance to get out of the country."

"We wouldn't have to hide. Jesu Cristo, who would know we did it?" chipped in Sebastian roughly.

"Everybody will know it soon. You made a bad mistake when you didn't bump me off at the start. All your friends that helped bushwhack me will itch to get that five hundred, Sebastian. As to hiding—well, I was a ranger once. Offer a reward, and everybody is on the jump to earn it. The way these hills are being combed this week by anxious man-hunters you'd never reach your cache."

"Maybe we would and maybe we wouldn't. We'll have to take a chance on that," replied the bearded Mexican sullenly.

To their prisoner it was plain that the men were I growing more anxious every hour. They regretted the course they had followed and yet could see no way of safety opening to them. Suspicious by nature, Sebastian judged the American by himself. If their positions were reversed, he knew he would break any pledge he might make and go straight to the sheriff with his story. Therefore they could not with safety release the man. To kill him would be dangerous. To keep him prisoner was possible only for a limited time. Whatever course they followed seemed precarious and uncertain. Temperamentally he was inclined to put an end to the man and try a bolt for the hills, but he found in Pablo an unexpected difficulty. The young man would not hear of this. He had made up his mind riot to let Gordon be killed if he could prevent it, though he did not tell the American so.

Menendez made another trip after supplies next day, but he came back hurriedly without them. Pesquiera's poster offering a reward of one hundred dollars for the capture of him or Sebastian had brought him up short and sent him scurrying back to his hole.

Gordon used the poster for a text. His heart was jubilant within him, for he knew now that Valencia was not back of this attack upon him.

"All up with you now," he assured them in a genial, offhand fashion. "Miss Valdes must be backing Pesquiera. They know you two are the guilty villains. Inside of twelve hours they'll have you both hogtied."

Clearly the conspirators were of that opinion themselves. They talked together a good deal in whispers. Dick was of the opinion that a proposition would be made him before morning, though it was just possible that the scale might tip the other way and his death be voted. He spent a very anxious hour.

After dark Sebastian, who was less well known in the town than Pablo, departed on an errand unknown to Gordon. The miner guessed that he was going to make arrangements for horses upon which to escape. Dick was not told their decision. Menendez had fallen sulky again and refused to talk.

CHAPTER XVIII

MANUEL INTERFERES

Valencia had scarcely left the parlor to telephone for the sheriff before Manuel flashed a knife and cut the rope that tied his prisoner's hands.

Sebastian had shrunk back at sight of the knife, but when he found that he was free he stared at Pesquiera in startled amazement.

"Come! Let's get out of here. We can talk when you are free of danger," said Manuel with sharp authority in his voice.

He led the way into the corridor, walked quickly down one passage and along another, and so by a back stairway into the alley in the rear. Within a few minutes they were a quarter of a mile from the El Tovar.

Sebastian, still suspicious, yet aware that for some reason Don Manuel was unexpectedly on his side, awaited explanations.

"*Dona* Valdes is quite right, Sebastian. She means well, but she is, after all, a woman. This is a man's business, and you and I can settle it better alone." Manuel smiled with an air of frank confidence at his former prisoner. "You are in a serious fix—no doubt at all about that. The question is to find the best way out."

"Si, Senor".

Pesquiera's bright black eyes fastened on him as he flung a question at the man. "I suppose this Gordon is still alive."

Sebastian nodded gloomily. "He is like a cat with its nine lives. We have beaten and starved him, but he laughs—this Gringo devil—and tells us he will live to see us wearing stripes in prison."

"Muy bien." Manuel talked on briskly, so as to give the slower-witted Mexican no time to get set in obstinacy. "I should be able to arrange matters then. We must free the man after I have his word to tell nothing."

"But he will run straight to the sheriff," protested Sebastian.

"Not if he gives his word. I'll see to that. Where have you him hidden?" The young Spaniard asked the question carelessly, almost indifferently, as if it were merely a matter of course.

Sebastian opened his mouth to tell—and then closed it. He had had no intention of telling anything. Now he found he had told everything except their hiding-place. The suspicion which lay coiled in his heart lifted its head like a snake. Was he being led into a trap? Would Don Manuel betray him to the law? The gleaming eyes of the man narrowed and grew hard.

Manuel, intuitively sensing this, hurried on. "It can be a matter of only hours now until they stumble upon your hiding-place. If this happens before we have come to terms with Gordon you are lost. I have come to town to save you and Pablo. But I can't do this unless you trust me. Take me to Gordon and let me talk with him. Blindfold me if you like. But lose no time."

As Sebastian saw it, this was a chance. He knew Manuel was an honest man. His reputation was of the best. Reluctantly he gave way.

"The *Americano* is at the Valdes house," he admitted sulkily.

"At the Valdes house? Why, in Heaven's name, did you take him there?"

"How could we tell that the *Senorita* would come to town? The house was empty. Pablo worked there in the stables as a boy. So we moved in."

A quarter of an hour later Pablo opened the outer basement door in answer to the signal agreed upon by them. He had left the prisoner upon the bed with his hands tied. Sebastian entered. Pablo noticed that another man was standing outside. Instantly his rifle covered him. For, though others of their countrymen had been employed to help capture Gordon, none of these knew where he was hidden.

"It is Don Manuel Pesquiera," explained Sebastian. "I brought him here to help us out of this trouble we are in. Let him in and I will tell you all."

For an instant Pablo suspected that his accomplice had sold him, but he dismissed the thought almost at once. He had known Sebastian all his life. He stepped aside and let Pesquiera come into the hall.

The three men talked for a few minutes and then passed into the bedroom where the prisoner was confined. Evidently this had formerly been the apartment of the cook, who had slept in the basement in order no doubt to be nearer her work. Pesquiera looked around and at last made out a figure in the darkness lying upon the bed.

He stepped forward, observing that the man on the bed had his hands bound. Bending down, he recognized the face of Gordon. Beaten and bruised and gaunt from hunger it was, but the eyes still gleamed with the same devil-may-care smile.

"Happy to meet you, Don Manuel."

The Spaniard's heart glowed with admiration. He did not like the man. It was his intention to fight him as soon as possible for the insult that had been put upon him some weeks earlier. But his spirit always answered to the call of courage, and Gordon's pluck was so debonair he could not refuse a reluctant appreciation.

"I regret to see you thus, Mr. Gordon," he said.

"Might have been worse. Sebastian has had se-vere-al notions about putting me out of business. I'm lucky to be still kicking."

"I have come from Miss Valdes. She came to Santa Fe when she heard from your friend Mr. Davis that you had disappeared. To-night we saw Sebastian for the first time. He brought me here."

"Good of him," commented Dick ironically.

"You will be freed of course—at once." Manuel drew out his

knife and cut the cords that bound the prisoner. "But I must ask your forbearance in behalf of Sebastian and Pablo and the others that have injured you. May I give them your pledge not to appear as a witness against them for what they have done?"

"Fine! I'm to be mauled and starved and kidnaped, but I'm to say 'Thank you kindly' for these small favors, hoping for a continuance of the same. You have another guess coming, Mr. Pesquiera. I offered those terms two days ago. They weren't accepted. My ideas have changed. I'm going to put your friends behind the bars—unless you decide to let them murder me instead. I've been the goat long enough."

"Your complaint is just, Mr. Gordon. It iss your right to enforce the law. Most certainly it iss your right. But consider my position. Sebastian brought me here only upon my pledge to secure from you a promise not to press your rights. What shall I do? I must see that you are released. That goes without saying. But shall I break faith with him and let him be delivered to justice? I have given my word, remember."

Gordon looked up at him with his lean jaw set. "You couldn't give *my* word, could you? Very well. Go away. Forget that you've seen me. I'll be a clam so far as you are concerned. But if I get free I'm going to make things hot for these lads that think they can play Ned with me. They're going to the pen, every last one of them. I'm going to see this thing out to a finish and find out if there's any law in New Mexico."

Manuel stiffened. "You put me in an awkward position, Mr. Gordon. I have no choice but to see you are set at liberty. But my honor is involved. These men shall not go to prison. They have made a serious mistake, but they are not what you call criminals. You know well—"

"I know that they and their friends have shot at me, ambushed me, beaten me, and starved me. They've been wanting to kill me ever since they got me here—at least one of them has—but they just didn't have the guts to do it. What is your definition of a criminal anyhow? Your friends here fill the specifications close enough to suit me. I ain't worried about their being too good for the company they'll join at the pen."

"You are then resolve', *Senor*?"

"That's what I am. I'm going to see they get the limit. I've not got a thing against you, Mr. Pesquiera, and I'd like to oblige you if I could. But I'm playing this hand myself."

The Spaniard spoke to him in a low voice. "These men are the people of Miss Valdes. She drove all night across the mountains to get here sooner when she found you were gone. She offered and paid a reward of one hundred dollars to help find you. Do you not owe something to her?"

"I owe one hundred dollars and my thanks, sir. I'll pay them both. But Miss Valdes cannot ask me to give up prosecuting these men because she would not stand back and see murder done."

"Will you then leave it to her to punish these men?"

"No. I pay my own debts."

Manuel was troubled. He had expected to find the prisoner so eager for release that he would consent at once to his proposal. Instead, he found a man hard and cold as steel. Yet he had to admit that Gordon claimed only his rights. No man could be expected to stand without an appeal to the law such outrageous treatment as he had been given.

"Will you consent then to settle the matter with me, man to man? These men are but peons. They are like cattle and do not think. But I—I am a more worthy foeman. Let me take the burden of their misdeeds on my shoulders."

Dick wagged a forefinger at him warningly. "Now you've got that swashbuckler notion of a duel again. I'm no cavalier of Spain, but a plain American business man, Don Quixote. As for these jail-birds"—his hand swept the room to include the Mexicans—"since I'm an unregenerate human I mean to make 'em pay for what they've done. That's all there is to it."

Don Manuel bowed. "Very good, Mr. Gordon. We shall see. I promise you that I shall stand between them and prison. I offer you a chance to win the friendship of the Mexicans in the valley. You decline. So be it. I wash my hands, sir."

He turned away and gave directions to Pablo, who left the room at once. The Spaniard called for candles and lit two. He pointedly ignored Gordon, but sat with his hands in his pockets whistling softly a popular air.

About a quarter of an hour later Pablo returned with a hot meal on a tray. Gordon, having done without food for two days, ate his ham and eggs and drank his coffee with an appetite given to few men. Meanwhile Pesquiera withdrew to the passage and laid down an ultimatum to the Mexicans. They must take horse at once and get back to the hills above the Rio Chama Valley. He would bring saddle horses from a stable so that they could start within the hour and travel all night.

The Mexicans listened sullenly. But they knew that the matter was now out of their hands. Since the arrival of Pesquiera it had become manifestly impossible to hold their prisoner longer. They agreed to the plan of the Spaniard reluctantly.

After Pablo and Sebastian had taken horse Pesquiera returned to the prisoner.

"We will, if it pleases you, move upstairs, Mr. Gordon," he announced. "To-night I must ask you to remain in the house with me to give those poor fools a little start on their ride for freedom. We shall find better beds upstairs no doubt."

"They're hitting the trail, are they?" Dick asked negligently as he followed his guide.

"Yes. If you'll give me your parole till morning, Mr. Gordon, I shall be able to return to Miss Valdes and let her know that all is well. Otherwise I shall be obliged to sit up and see that you do not get active in interfering with the ride of Pablo and his friend."

"I'll stay here till seven o'clock to-morrow morning. Is that late enough? Then I'll see the sheriff and start things moving."

Pesquiera bowed in his grand, formal manner. "The terms satisfy. I wish Mr. Gordon a very good night's sleep. This room formerly belonged to the brother of Miss Valdes. It is curious, but she was here airing this room only to-day. She did not know you were in the house at the time. *Adios, Senor.*"

"Good night, Mr. Pesquiera. I reckon I'm in your debt quite a bit. Sorry we couldn't agree about this little matter of what to do with the boys."

Manuel bowed again and withdrew from the room.

Inside of ten minutes Gordon was fast asleep.

CHAPTER XIX

VALENCIA ACCEPTS A RING

Manuel found Valencia pacing up and down the porch of the hotel in a fever of impatience. Instantly at sight of him she ran forward quickly.

"Where have you been? What have you done with Sebastian? Why did you leave without telling me about it?" she demanded.

"One question at a time, my cousin," he answered, smiling at her. "But let us walk while I tell you."

She fell into step beside him, moving with the strong, lissom tread that came from controlled and deliberate power.

"What is it you have to tell? If you were called away, why did you not leave a message for me?" she asked, a little imperiously.

"I wasn't called away, Valencia. You were excited and angry. My opinion was that Sebastian would speak if the matter was put to him right. So I cut the rope that tied him and we ran away through the back door of the hotel."

Her dark eyes, proud and passionate, began to smoulder. But the voice with which she answered him was silken smooth.

"I see. You pretended to be working with me—and then you betrayed me. Is that it?"

"If you like," he said with a little shrug. "I backed my judgment against your impatience. And it turns out that I was right."

"How? What has happened? Where is Sebastian?"

"He is galloping toward the hills as fast as he can—at least I hope he is. What happened is that he told me where Gordon is hidden."

"Where?"

"At your house. When you were there to-day you must have passed within twenty feet of him."

"But—do you mean that Pablo and Sebastian took him there?"

"Exactly. They did not foresee that you would come to town, Valencia." He added, after a moment: "I have seen Mr. Gordon, talked with him, and released him. At this moment he is in your brother's room, probably asleep."

All the sharpness had died out of the young woman's voice when she turned to her cousin and spoke with a humility rare to her.

"Forgive me, Manuel. I always know best about everything. I drive ahead and must have my own way, even when it is not the wise one. You did just right to ignore me."

She laid her hand on his coat sleeve pleadingly, and he lifted it to his lips.

"*Nina*... the Queen can do no wrong. But I saw you were driving Sebastian to stubbornness. I tried to let him see we meant to be his friends if he would let us."

"Yes, you were right. Tell me everything, please." She paused just a moment before she said quietly: "But first, what about Mr. Gordon? He is... uninjured?"

"Beaten and mauled and starved, but still of the gayest courage," answered the Spaniard with enthusiasm. "Did I not say that he was a hero? My cousin, I say it again. The fear of death is not in his heart."

He did not see the gleam in her dark eyes, the flush that beat into her dusky face. "Starved as well as beaten, Manuel?"

"They were trying to force him to give up his claim to the valley. But he—as I live the American is hard as Gibraltar."

"They dared to starve him—to torture him. I shall see that they are punished," she cried with the touch of feminine ferocity that is the heritage of the south.

"No need, Valencia," returned Pesquiera with a dry little laugh. "Mr. Gordon has promised himself to attend to that."

He told her the story from first to last. Intently she listened, scarce breathing until he had finished.

Manuel had told the tale with scrupulous fairness, but already her sympathies were turning.

"And he wouldn't agree not to prosecute?" she asked.

"No. It is his right to do so if he likes, Valencia."

She brushed this aside with an impatient wave of her hand. "Oh, his right! Doesn't he owe something to us—to me—and especially to you?"

"No, he owes me nothing. What I did was done for you, and not for him," the Spaniard replied instantly.

"Then to me at least he is in debt. I shall ask him to drop the prosecution."

"He is what his people call straight. But he is hard—hard as jade."

They were walking along a dark lane unlighted save by the stars. Valencia turned to him impetuously.

"Manuel, you are good. You do not like this man, but you save him because—because my heart is torn when my people do wrong. For me you take much trouble—you risk much. How can I thank you?"

"*Nina mia*, I am thanked if you are pleased. It is your love I seek, Heart of mine." He spoke tremulously, taking her hands in his.

For the beat of a heart she hesitated. "You have it. Have I not given my word that—after the American was saved—?"

He kissed her. Hers was a virginal soul, but full-blooded. An unsuspected passion beat in her veins. Not for nothing did she have the deep, languorous eyes, the perfect scarlet lips, the sumptuous grace of an artist's ideal. Fires lay banked within her in spite of the fine purity of her nature. Nature had poured into her symmetrical mold a rich abundance of what we call sex.

The kisses of Manuel stirred within her new and strange emotions, though she accepted rather than returned them. A faint vague unease chilled her heart. Was it because she had been immodest in letting him so far have his way?

When they returned to the hotel Manuel's ring was on her finger. She was definitely engaged to him.

It was long before she slept. She thought of Manuel, the man chosen it seemed by Fate to be her mate. But she thought, too, of the lithe, broad-shouldered young American whose eyes could be so tender and again so hard. Why was it he persisted in filling her mind so much of the time? Why did she both admire him and resent his conduct, trust him to the limit one hour and distrust the next? Why was it that he—an unassuming American without any heroics—rather than her affianced lover seemed to radiate romance as he moved? She liked Manuel very much, she respected him greatly, trusted him wholly, but—it was this curly-headed youth of her mother's race that set her heart beating fast a dozen times a day.

She resolved resolutely to put him out of her mind. Had he not proved himself unworthy by turning the head of Juanita, whom he could not possibly expect to marry? Was not Manuel in every way worthy of her love? Her finger touched the diamond ring upon her hand. She would keep faith in thought as well as in word and deed.

At last she fell asleep—and dreamed of a blond, gray-eyed youth fighting for his life against a swarm of attacking Mexicans.

CHAPTER XX

DICK LIGHTS A CIGARETTE

Gordon met Miss Valdes in the El Tovar dining-room next morning. He was trying at the same time to tell Davis the story of his kidnaping and to eat a large rare steak with French-fried potatoes. The young man had chosen a seat that faced the door. The instant his eyes fell upon her he gave up both the story and the steak. Putting aside his napkin, he rose to meet her.

She had fallen asleep thinking of him, her dreams had been full of his vivid personality, and she had wakened to an eager longing for the sight of his gay, mocking eyes. But she had herself under such good control that nobody could have guessed how fast her heart was beating as her fingers touched his.

"We are glad your adventure is ended, Mr. Gordon, and that it has turned out no worse. Probably Mr. Davis has told you that he and I got our heads together a great many times a day," she said, a little formally.

"You were mighty good to take so much interest in such a scalawag," he answered warmly.

The color deepened ever so little in her face. "I couldn't let my men commit murder under the impression they were doing me a service," she explained lightly. "There are several things I want to talk over with you. Can you call on me this morning, Mr. Gordon?"

"Can I?"

He put the question so forcefully that she smiled and dashed a bucket of cold water over his enthusiasm.

"If you'll be so good then. And bring Mr. Davis along with you, please. He'll keep us from quarreling too much."

"I'll throw him out of the window if he don't behave right," Davis promised joyfully. He was happy to-day, and he did not care who knew it.

Valencia passed on to her table, and Dick resumed his seat. He had a strong interest in this young woman, but even the prospect of a talk with her could not make him indifferent to the rare steak and French-fried potatoes before him. He was a healthy normal American in his late twenties, and after several days of starvation well-cooked food looked very good to him.

"There's some mail waiting for you upstairs—one of the letters is a registered one, mailed at Corbett's," his friend told him as they rose to leave. He was like a hen with one chick in his eagerness to supply Dick's wants and in his reluctance to let Gordon out of his sight.

The registered letter was the one Valencia had sent him, inclosing the one written by her grandfather to her father. Her contrite little note went straight to his emotions. If not in words, at least in spirit, it pleaded for pardon. Even the telegram she had wired implied an undeniable interest in him. Dick went with a light heart to the interview she had appointed him.

He slipped an arm through that of Davis. "Come on, you old bald-headed chaperone. Didn't you hear the lady give you a bid to her party this mo'ning? Get a move on you."

"Ain't you going to let her invite get cold before you butt in?" retorted Steve amiably.

Valencia took away from the dining-room a heart at war with itself. The sight of his gaunt face, carrying the scars of many wounds and the lines marked by hunger, stirred insurgent impulses. The throb of passion and of the sweet protective love that is at the bottom of every woman's tenderness suffused her cheeks with warm life and made her eyes wonderful. Out of the grave he had come back to her, this indomitable foe who played the game with such gay courage. It was useless to tell herself that she was plighted to a better man, a worthier one. Scamp he might be, but Dick Gordon held her heart in the hollow of his strong brown hand.

Some impulse of shyness, perhaps of reluctance, had restrained her from wearing Manuel's ring at breakfast. But when she returned to her room she went straight to the desk where she had locked it and put the solitaire on her finger. The fear of disloyalty drove her back to her betrothed from the enticement of forbidden thoughts. She must put Richard Gordon out of her mind. It was worse than madness to be dreaming of him now that she was plighted to another.

Gordon, coming eagerly to meet her, found a young woman more reserved, more distant. He was conscious of this even before his eyes stopped at the engagement ring sparkling on her finger, the visible evidence that his rival had won.

"You have been treated cruelly, Mr. Gordon. Tell me that you are again all right," she said, the color flooding her face at the searching question of his eyes.

"Right as a rivet, thanks. It is to you I owe my freedom, I suppose."

"To Manuel," she corrected. "His judgment was better than mine."

"I can believe that. He didn't ride all night across dangerous mountain roads to save me."

"Oh, that!" She tossed off his thanks with a little shrug. "They are so impulsive, my boys... like children, you know.... I was a little afraid they might—"

"I was a little afraid myself they might," he agreed dryly. "But when you say children—well, don't you think wolves is a more accurate term for them?"

"Oh, no—no!" Her protest was quick, eager, imperative. "You don't know how loyal they can be—how faithful. They are really just like children, so impulsive—so unreasoning."

"Afraid I can't enthuse with you on that subject for a day or two yet," he answered with a laugh. "Truth is I found their childlike impulses both painful and annoying. Next time you see them you might mention that I'm liable to have an impulse of my own they won't enjoy."

"That's one of the things I want to talk with you about. Manuel says you mean to prosecute. I hope you won't. They're friends of mine. They thought they were helping me. Of course I have no claim on you, but—"

"You have a claim, Miss Valdes. We'll take that up presently. Just now we're talking about a couple of criminals due for a term in the penitentiary. I offered them terms. They wouldn't accept. Good enough. They'll have to stand the gaff, I reckon."

She realized at once there was no use arguing with him. The steel in his eyes told her he had made up his mind and was not to be moved. But she could not desert her foolish dependents.

"I know. What you say is quite true, but—I'll have to come to some agreement with you. I can't let them be punished for their loyalty to me."

Her direct, unflinching look, its fearlessness, won his admiration. In her slim suppleness, vibrant, feminine to the finger tips, alluring with the unconscious appeal of sex, there was a fine courage to face frankly essential facts. But he was a hard man to move once he had made up his mind. For all his frivolous impudence and his boyish good nature, he knew his own mind, and held to it with the stiffness characteristic of outdoor Westerners.

"You're not in this, Miss Valdes. I'll settle my own accounts with your friends Sebastian and Pablo."

"But even for your own sake—" She stopped, intuitively aware that this was not the ground upon which to treat with him. He would never drop the charges against the Mexicans merely because there was danger in pressing them.

"I reckon I'll have to try to look out for myself. Maybe next time I won't be so easy a mark," he answered with an almost insolent laugh.

Valencia was a little puzzled. Things were not going right,

and she did not quite know the reason. There was just a touch of bitterness in his voice, of aloofness in his manner. She did not know that the sight of the solitaire sparkling on her left hand stirred in him the impulse to hurt her, to refuse rather than concede her requests.

"You're not going to push the cases against Pablo and Sebastian and still try to live in the valley, are you?" she asked, beginning to feel a little irritation at him.

"That's just what I'm going to do."

"You mustn't. I won't have it. Don't you see what my people will think, that because Pablo and Sebastian were loyal to me—"

His acrid smile cut her sentence in two. "That's about the third time you've mentioned their loyalty. Me, I don't see it. Sebastian owns land under the Valdes grant. He didn't want me to take it from him. Mr. Pablo Menendez—well, he had private reasons of his own, too."

The resentment flamed in her heart. If he was shameless enough to refer to the affair with Juanita she would let him know that she knew.

"What were his reasons, Mr. Gordon—that is, if they are not a private affair between you and him?"

"Not at all." The steel-blue eyes met hers, steadily. Dick was yielding to a desire to hurt himself as well as her, to defy her judgment if she had no better sense than to condemn him. "The idiot is jealous."

"Jealous—why?" The angry color beat its way to the surface above her cheek bones. Her disdain was regal.

"About Juanita."

"What about Juanita?"

"The usual thing, Miss Valdes. He was afraid she had the bad taste to prefer another man to himself."

Davis broke in. "Now, don't you be a goat, Dick. Miss Valdes, he—"

"If you please, Mr. Davis. I'm quite sure Mr. Gordon is able to defend himself," she replied scornfully.

"Didn't know I *was* defending myself. What's the charge against me?" asked the young miner with a touch of quiet insolence.

"There isn't any—if you don't see what it is. And you're quite right, Mr. Gordon. Your difficulties with Pablo are none of my business. You'll have to settle them yourselves—with Juanita's help. May I ask whether you received the registered letter I sent you, Mr. Gordon?"

Dick was angry. Her cool contempt told him that he had been condemned. He knew that he was acting like an irresponsible schoolboy, but he would not justify himself. She might think what she liked.

"Found it waiting for me this morning, Miss Valdes."

"It was very fair and generous of you to send me the letter, I recognize that fully. But of course I can't accept such a sacrifice," she told him stiffly.

"Not necessary you should. Object if I smoke here?"

Valencia was a little surprised. He had never before offered to smoke in the house except at her suggestion. "As you please, Mr. Gordon. Why should I object?"

From his coat pocket Dick took the letter Don Bartolome had written to his son, and from his vest pocket a match. He twisted the envelope into a spill, lit one end, and found a cigarette. Very deliberately he puffed the cigarette to a glow, holding the letter in his fingers until it had burned to a black flake. This he dropped in the fireplace, and along with it the unsmoked cigarette.

"Easiest way to settle that little matter," he said negligently.

"I judge you're a little impulsive, too, sometimes, Mr. Gordon," Valencia replied coldly.

"I never rode all night over the mountains to save a man who was trying to rob me of my land," he retorted.

This brought a sparkle to her eyes. "I had to think of my foolish men who were getting into trouble."

"Was that why you offered a hundred dollars' reward for the arrest of these same men?" came his indolent, satiric reply.

"Don Manuel offered the reward," she told him haughtily.

An impish smile was in his eyes. "At your suggestion, he tells me. And I understand you insisted on paying the bill, Miss Valdes."

"Why should he pay it? The men worked for me. They were brought up on my father's place. They are my responsibility, not his," she claimed with visible irritation.

"And now they're my responsibility, too—until I land them in the penitentiary," he added cheerfully.

From his pocket he took a billbook and selected two fifty-dollar bills. These he offered to Valencia.

She stood very straight. "You owe me nothing, sir."

"I owe you the hundred dollars you paid to get hold of Sebastian. And I'm going to pay it."

"I don't acknowledge the debt. I wanted Sebastian for his sake, not yours. Certainly I shall not accept the money."

"Just as you say. It isn't mine. Care if I smoke again?" he asked genially.

She caught his meaning in a flash. "Not at all. Burn them if you like."

"Now, see here," interrupted Davis amiably. "You're both acting like a pair of kids. I'm not going to stand for any hundred-dollar smokes, Dick. Gimme those bills." He snatched them from his friend and put them in his pocket. "When you two get reasonable again we'll decide whose money it is. Till then I expect I'll draw the interest on it."

"And now, since our business is ended, I think I'll not detain you any longer, Mr. Gordon, except to warn you that it will be foolhardy to return to the Rio Chama Valley with intentions such as you have."

"Good of you to warn me, Miss Valdes. It's not the first time, either, is it? But I'm *that* bull-headed. Steve will give me a recommend as the most sot chump in New Mexico. Won't you Steve?"

"I sure will—before a notary if you like. You've got a government mule backed off the map."

"I've done my duty, anyhow." Miss Valdes turned to the older man, and somehow the way she did it seemed to wipe Gordon out of the picture. "There is something I want to talk over with you, Mr. Davis. Can you wait a few moments?"

"Sure I can—all day if you like."

Dick retired with his best bow. "Steve, you always was popular with the ladies."

Valencia, uncompromising, waited until he had gone. Then, swiftly, with a little leap of impulse as it were, she appealed to Davis.

"Don't let him go back to the valley. Don't let him push the cases against Sebastian and Pablo."

The old miner shook his head "Sorry, Miss Valencia. Wish I could stop him, but I can't. He'll go his own way—always would."

"But don't you see they'll kill him. It's madness to go back there while he's pushing the criminal case. Before it was bad enough, but now—" She threw up her hands with a gesture of despair.

"I reckon you're right. But I can't help it."

"Then look out for him. Don't let him ride around in the hills. Don't let him leave the house at night. Never let him go alone. Remember that he is in danger every hour while he remains in the valley."

"I'll remember, Miss Valencia," Davis promised.

He wondered as he walked away why the talk between Dick and Miss Valdes had gone so badly. He knew his friend had come jubilantly, prepared to do anything she asked of him. The fear and anxiety that had leaped to her face the instant Gordon had gone showed him that the girl had a deep interest in the young man. She, too, had meant to meet him half way in wiping out the gulf between them. Instead, they had only increased it.

CHAPTER XXI

WHEN THE WIRES WERE CUT

Don Manuel rode into the moonlit plaza of the Valdes ranch, dismounted, and flung the reins to the boy that came running. Pesquiera nodded a careless greeting and passed into the house. He did not ask of anyone where Valencia was, nor did he send in a card of announcement. A lover's instinct told him that he would find her in the room that served both as an office and a library for her, seated perhaps before the leaping fireglow she loved or playing softly on the piano in the darkness.

The door was open, and he stood a moment on the threshold to get accustomed to the dim light.

A rich, low-pitched voice came across the room to him.

"It is you, Manuel?"

He stepped swiftly forward to the lounge upon which she was lying and knelt on one knee beside her, lifting her hand to his lips. "It is I, *corazon mia*, even Manuel the lucky."

She both smiled and sighed at that. A chord in her responded to the extravagance of his speech, even though vaguely it did not quite satisfy. A woman of the warm-blooded south and no plaster saint, she answered presently with shy, reluctant lips the kisses of her lover. Why should she not? Had he not won her by meeting the test she had given him? Was he not a gallant gentleman, of her own race and caste, bound to her by ties of many sorts, in every way worthy to be the father of her children? If she had to stifle some faint, indefinable regret, was it not right that she should? Her bridges were burned behind her. He was the man of her choice. She listened, eyes a little wistful, while he poured out ardently the tale of his devotion.

"You do love me, don't you, Manuel?" she demanded, a little fiercely. It was as if she wanted to drown any doubts she might have of her own feeling in the certainty of his.

"More than life itself, I do believe," he cried in a low voice.

Her lithe body turned, so that her shining eyes were close to his.

"Dear Manuel, I am glad. You don't know how worried I've been... still am. Perhaps if I were a man it would be different, but I don't want my people to take the life of this stranger. But they mean him harm—especially since he has come back and intends to punish Pablo and Sebastian. I want them to let the law take its course. Something tells me that we shall win in the end. I've talked to them—and talked—but they say nothing except 'Si, dona.' But with you to help me—"

"They'd better not touch him again," broke in her lover swiftly.

"It's a great comfort to me, Manuel, that you have blotted out your own quarrel with him. It was magnanimous, what I should expect of you."

He said nothing, but the hand that lay on hers seemed suddenly to stiffen. A kind of fear ran shivering through her. Quickly she rose from the couch.

"Manuel, tell me that I am right, that you don't mean to... hurt him?" Her dark eyes searched his unflinchingly. "You don't mean... you can't mean... that—?"

"Let us forget the American and remember only that we love, my beloved," he pleaded.

"No... No!" The voice of the girl was sharp and imperative. "I want the truth. Is it that you are still thinking of murdering him, Manuel?"

The sting of her words brought a flush to his cheeks. "I fight fair, Valencia. I set against his life my own, with all the happiness that has come flooding it. Nor is it that I seek the man's life. For me he might live a thousand years—and welcome. But my honor—"

"No, Manuel. No—no—no! I will not have it. If you are betrothed to me your life is mine. You shall not risk it in a barbarous duel."

"Let us change the subject, dear heart."

"Not till I hear you say that you have given up this wicked intention of yours."

He gave up the attempt to evade her and met her fairly as one man does another.

"I can't say that, Valencia, not even for you. This quarrel lies between him and me. I have suffered humiliation and disgrace. Until those are wiped out there must be war

William MacLeod Raine

between me and the American."

"Since the day I first wore your ring, Manuel, I have asked nothing of you. I ask now that you will forget the slight this man has put upon you... because I ask it of you with all my heart."

A slight tremor ran through his blood. He felt himself slipping from his place with her.

"I can't, Valencia. You don't know what you ask, how impossible it is for me—a Pesquiera, son of my honored fathers—to grant such a request." He stretched his hands toward her imploringly.

"Yet you say you love me?"

"Heaven knows whether it is not true, my cousin."

"You want me to believe that, even though you refuse the first real request I ever made of you?"

"Anything else in the world that is in my power."

"It is easy to say that, Manuel, when it isn't something else I want. Give me this American's life. I shall know, then, that you love me."

"You know now," he answered quietly.

"Is love all sighs and vows?" she cried impatiently. "Will it not sacrifice pride and vanity for the object of its devotion?"

"Everything but honor," answered the man steadfastly.

She made a gesture of despair.

"What is this honor you talk so much about? It is neither Christian nor lawful nor right."

"It is a part of me, Valencia."

"Then your ideas are archaic. The duel was for a time when every man had to seek his personal redress. There is law in this twentieth century."

"Not as between man and man in the case of a personal indignity—at least, not for Manuel Pesquiera."

"But it is so needless. We know you are brave; he knows it, too. Surely your vanity—"

He smiled a little sadly.

"I think it is not vanity, but something deeper. None of my ancestors could have tolerated this stigma, nor can their son. My will has nothing to do with it, and my desire still less. It is kismet."

"Then you must know the truth—that if you kill this man I can never—"

"Never what?"

"Never marry you."

"Why?"

"His blood would stand between us."

"Do you mean that you—love him?"

Her dark eyes met his steadily.

"I don't think I mean that, Manuel. How could I mean that, since I love you and am betrothed to you? Sometimes I hate him. He is so insolent in his daring. Then, too, he is my enemy, and he has come here to set this happy valley to hate and evil. Yet, if I should hurt him, it would stand between us forever."

"I am sorry."

"Only sorry, Manuel?"

He clamped his teeth on the torrent of protest that rose within him when she handed him back his ring. It would do no good to speak more. The immutable fact stood between them.

"I did not know life could be so hard—and cruel," she cried out in a burst of passion.

She went to the open window and looked out upon the placid, peaceful valley. She had a swift, supple way of moving, as if her muscles responded with effortless ease to her volition; but the young man noticed that to-night there was a drag to her motions.

His heart yearned toward her. He longed mightily to take her in his arms and tell her that he would do as she wished. But, as he had said, something in him more potent than vanity, than pride, than his will, held him to the course he had set for himself. His views of honor might be archaic and ridiculous, but he lived by his code as tenaciously as had his fathers. Gordon had insulted and humiliated him publicly. He must apologize or give him satisfaction. Until he had done one or the other Manuel could not live at peace with himself. He had put a powerful curb upon his desire to wait as long as he had. Circumstances had for a time taken the matter out of his hands, but the time had come when he meant to press his claims. The American might refuse the duel; he could not refrain from defending himself when Pesquiera attacked.

A step sounded in the doorway, and almost simultaneously a voice.

"*Dona,* are you here?"

The room was lighted only by the flickering fire; but Valencia, her eyes accustomed to the darkness, recognized the boy as Juan Gardiez.

"Yes, I am here, Juan. What have you to tell me?" she said quickly.

"I do not know, *senorita.* But the men—Pablo, Sebastian; all of them—are gone."

"Gone where?" she breathed.

"I do not know. To-day I drove a cow and calf to Willow Springs. I am but returned. The houses are empty. Senor Barela's wife says she saw men riding up the hill toward Corbett's—eight, nine, ten of them."

"To Corbett's?" She stared whitely at him without moving. "How long ago?"

"An hour ago—or more."

"Saddle Billy at once and bring him round," the girl ordered crisply.

She turned as she spoke and went lightly to the telephone. With the need of action, of decision, her hopelessness was gone. There was a hard, bright light in her eyes that told of a resolution inflexible as tempered steel when once aroused.

"Give me Corbett's—at once, please. Hallo, Central—Corbett's—"

No answer came, though she called again and again.

"There must be something wrong with the telephone," suggested Don Manuel.

She dropped the receiver and turned quietly to him.

"The wires have been cut."

"But, why? What is it all about?"

"Merely that my men are anticipating you. They have gone to murder the American. Deputy sheriffs from Santa Fe to-day came here to arrest Pablo and Sebastian. The men suspected and were hidden. Now they have gone to punish Mr. Gordon for sending the officers."

She could not have touched him more nearly. He came to her with burning eyes.

"How do you know? What makes you think so?"

She told him, briefly and simply, giving more detailed reasons.

Without a word, he turned and left her. She could hear him rushing through the hall, traced his progress by the slamming of the door, and presently caught sight of him running toward the corral. He did not hear, or heed, her call for him to wait.

The girl hurried out of the house after him, in time to see him slap a saddle on his bronco, swing to his seat lightly, and gallop in a cloud of dust to the road.

Valencia waited for no more. Quickly running to her room, she slipped on a khaki riding-skirt. Her deft, tapering fingers moved swiftly, so that she was ready, crop in hand, booted and spurred, by the time Juan brought round her horse.

It took but an instant to lift herself to the saddle and send Billy galloping forward.

Already her cousin had disappeared in great clouds of dust over the brow of the hill.

William MacLeod Raine

CHAPTER XXII

THE ATTACK

Dick Gordon and Davis were sitting on the porch of their cabin, which was about an eighth of a mile from the main buildings of the Corbett place. They had returned the day before from Santa Fe, along with two deputy sheriffs who had come to arrest Pablo and Sebastian. The officers had scoured the valley for two days, and as yet had not caught a glimpse of the men they had come to get. Their inquiries were all met by a dogged ignorance on the part of the Mexicans, who had of a sudden turned surprisingly stupid. No, they had seen nothing of Pablo or of Sebastian. They knew nobody of that name—unless it was old Pablo Gardiez the *senors* wished to see. Many strangers desired to see him, for he was more than a hundred years old and still remembered clearly the old days.

Gordon laughed at the discomfiture of his sleuths. "I dare say they may have been talking to the very men they wanted. But everybody hangs together in this valley. I'm going out with them myself to-morrow after the gentlemen the law requires."

"No, I wouldn't do that, Dick. With every greaser in the valley simmering against you, it won't do for you to go trapsing right down among them," Davis explained.

"That's where I'm going, anyhow—to-morrow morning. The deputies are staying up at Morrow's. I'm going to phone 'em to-night that I'll ride with them to-morrow. Bet you a new hat we flush our birds."

"What's the sense of you going into the police business, Dick? I'll tell you what's ailing you. You're just honing to see Miss Valdes again. You want to go grand-standing around making her mad at you some more."

"You're a wiz, Steve," admitted his friend dryly. "Maybe you're right. Maybe I do want to see her again. Why shouldn't I?"

"What good does it do you when you quarrel all the time you're together? She's declared herself already on this proposition—told the deputies flat-footed that she wouldn't tell them anything and would help her boys to escape in any way she could. You're just like a kid showing off his muscle before a little girl in the first grade."

"All right, Steve. You don't hear me denying it."

"Denying it," snapped the old miner. "Hmp! Lot of good that would do. You're fair itching to get a chance to go down to the ranch and swagger around in plain sight of her lads. You'd be tickled to death if you could cut out the two you want and land them here in spite of her and Don Manuel and the whole pack of them. Don't I know you? Nothing but vanity—that's all there's to it."

"He's off," murmured Dick with a grin to the scenery.

"You make me tired. Why don't you try a little horse sense

for a change? Honest, if you was a few years younger I'd put you acrost my knee and spank you."

Gordon lit a cigarette, but did not otherwise contribute to the conversation.

"Ain't she wearing another man's ring?" continued Davis severely. "What's bitin' you, anyhow? How many happy families you want to break up? First off, there's Pablo and Juanita. You fill up her little noodle with the notion that—"

Dick interrupted amiably. "Go to grass, you old granny. I've been putting in my spare time since I came back letting Juanita understand the facts. If she had any wrong notions she ain't got them any longer. She's all ready to kiss and make up with Pablo first chance she gets."

"Then there's Miss Valdes and this Pesky fellow, who's the whitest brown man I ever did see. Didn't he run his fool laigs off getting you free so you could go back and make love to his girl?"

"He's the salt of the earth. I'm for Don Manuel strong. But I don't reckon Miss Valdes would work well in harness with him," explained Dick.

Steve Davis snorted. "No, you reckon Dick Gordon would, though. Don't you see she's of his people—same customs, same ways, same—"

"She's no more of his people than she is of mine. Her mother was an American girl. She was educated in Washington. New Mexico is in America, not in Spain. Don't forget that, you old croaker."

"Well, she's engaged, ain't she? And to a good man. It ain't your put in."

"A good one, but the wrong one. It's a woman's privilege to change her mind. I'm here to help her change it," announced the young man calmly. "Say, look at Jimmie Corbett hitting the high spots this way."

Jimmie, not yet recovered from a severe fright, stopped to explain the adventure that had befallen him while he had been night fishing.

"I seen spooks, Mr. Gordon—hundreds of 'em—coming down the river bank on horseback—honest to goodness, I did."

"Jimmie, if I had your imagination—"

But Davis cut into Dick's smiling incredulity:

"Did you say on horseback, Jimmie?"

"Yes, sir, on horseback. Hope to die if they weren't—'bout fifty of them."

"You better run along home before they catch you, Jimmie," advised the old miner gravely.

The boy went like a streak of light. Davis turned quietly to his partner.

"I reckon it's come, Dick."

"You believe the boy did see some men on horseback? It might have been only shadows."

"No, sir. His imagination wouldn't have put spooks *on*

horseback. We got no time to argue. You going to hold the fort here or take to the hills?"

"You think they mean to attack us in the open?"

"They're hoping to surprise us, I reckon. That's why they're coming along the creek instead of the road. Hadn't 'a' been for Jimmie, they would have picked us off from the porch before we could say 'Jack Robinson.'"

Both men had at once stepped within the log cabin, and, as they talked, were strapping on ammunition belts and looking to their rifles and revolvers.

"There are too many doors and windows to this cabin. We can't hold it against them. We'll take the trail from the back door that leads up to the old spring. From up there we'll keep an eye on them," said Dick.

"I see 'em coming," cried the older man softly from the front window. "They ain't on the trail, but slipping up through the rocks. One—two—three—four—Lord, there's no end to the beggars! They're on foot now. Left their hawsses, I expect, down by the river."

Quietly the two men stepped from the back door of the cabin and swiftly ascended the little trail that rose at a sharp acclivity to the spring. At some height above the cabin, they crouched behind boulders and watched the cautious approach of the enemy.

"Not taking any chances, are they?" murmured Gordon.

Steve laughed softly.

"Heard about that chicken-killing affair, mebbe, and none of them anxious to add a goose to the exhibit."

"It would be right easy to give that surprise party a first-class surprise," chuckled Dick. "Shall I drop a pill or two down among them, just to let them know we're on the premises?"

"Now, don't you, Dick. We'll have to put half of 'em out of biz, and get shot up by the rest, if you do."

"All right. I'll be good, Steve. I was only joking, anyhow. But it ce'tainly is right funny to sit up here and watch them snake up to the empty cabin. See that fellow with the Mexican hat? I believe it's my jealous friend Pablo. He's ce'tainly anxious to get one Gringo's scalp. I could drop a stone down on him so he'd jump about 'steen feet."

"There's one reached the window. He's looking in mighty careful, you bet. Now he's beckoning the other fellows. I got a notion he's made a discovery."

"Got on to the fact that the nest's empty. They're pouring in like bees. Can you make out how many there are? I count nine," said Dick.

"They're having a powwow now. All talking with their hands, the way greasers do. Go to it, boys. A regular debating society, ain't you?"

"Hello! What's that mean?" broke in Gordon.

One of the Mexicans had left the rest, and was running toward the Corbett house.

"Gone to find whether we're on the porch with the family, up there," continued the young man, answering his own question.

"What's the matter with beating it while we've got a chanct?"

"I'm going to stay right here. You can go if you like, Steve?"

"Oh, well. I just suggested it." Davis helped himself to a chew of tobacco placidly.

"Fellow coming back from the house already," he presently added.

"Got the wrong address again. They'll be happening on the right one pretty soon."

"Soon as they're amply satisfied we ain't under the beds, or hid between the covers of some of them magazines. Blamed if they ain't lit a lamp."

Gordon gave a sudden exclamation of dismay. A Mexican had appeared at the back door of the cottage with a tin box in his hand.

"I'm the blamedest idiot out of an asylum," he cried bitterly. "All the proofs of my claim are in that box. You know I brought it back from Santa Fe with me."

"Ain't that too bad?"

Gordon rose, the lines of his mouth set fast and hard.

"I'm going down after it. If I lose those papers, the whole game's spoilt for me. I've got to have them, and I'm going to."

"Don't be a goat. How can you take it from a whole company of them?"

"I'll watch my chance. It may be the fellow will hide it

somewhere till he wants it again."

"I'm going, too, then."

"See here, Steve. Be sensible. If we both go down, it's a sure thing they will stumble on us."

"Too late, anyhow. They're coming up after us."

"So much the better. We'll cut across to the left, slip down, and take them in the rear. Likely as not we'll find it there."

"All right. Whatever you say, Dick."

They slipped away into the semi-darkness, taking advantage of every bit of cover they could find. Not until they were a long stone's throw from the trail did the young miner begin the descent.

Occasionally they could hear voices over to the right as they silently slipped down. It was no easy thing to negotiate that stiff mountainside in the darkness, where a slip would have sent one of them rolling down into the sharp rock-slide beneath. Presently they came to a rockrim, a sheer descent of twenty-five feet down the perpendicular face of a cliff.

They followed the ledge to the left, hoping to find a trough through which they might discover a way down. But in this they were disappointed.

"We'll have to go back. There's a place we passed where perhaps it may be done. We've got to try it, anyhow," said Gordon, in desperation.

Retracing their steps, they came to the point Dick had meant. It looked bad enough, in all conscience, but from the rocks there jutted halfway down a dwarf oak that had found rooting in a narrow cleft.

The young man worked his body over the edge, secured a foothold in some tiny scarp that broke the smoothness of the face, and groped, with one hand and then the other, for some hold that would do to brace his weight. He found one, lowered himself gingerly, and tested another foothold in a little bunch of dry moss.

"All right. My rifle, Steve."

It was handed down. At that precise moment there came to them the sound of approaching voices.

"Your gun, Steve! Quick. Now, then, over you come. That's right—no, the other hand—your foot goes there—easy, now."

They stood together on a three-inch ledge, their heels projecting over space. Nor had they reached this precarious safety any too soon, for already their pursuers were passing along the rim above.

One of them stopped on the edge, scarce eight feet above them.

"They must have come this way," he said to a companion. "But I expect they're hitting the trail about a mile from here."

"*Si, Pablo.* Can you feed me a cigareet?" the other asked.

The men below, scarce daring to breathe, waited, while the matches glimmered and the cigarettes puffed to a glow. Every instant they anticipated discovery; and they were in such a position that, if it came, neither of them could use his weapons. For they were cramped against the wall with their rifles by their sides, so bound by the situation that to have lifted them to aim would have been impossible.

"The American—he has escaped us this time," one of them said as they moved off.

"*Maldito*, the devil has given him wings to fly away," replied Pablo.

After the sound of their footsteps had died, Gordon resumed his descent. He reached the stunted oak in safety, and was again joined by his friend.

"Looks like we're caught here, Steve. There ain't a sign of a foothold below," the younger man whispered.

"Mebbe the branches of that tree will bend over."

"We'll have to try it, anyhow. If it breaks with me, I'll get to the bottom, just the same. Here goes."

Catching hold of the branches, he swung down and groped with his feet for a resting-place.

"Nothing doing, Steve."

"What blamed luck!"

"Hold on! Here's a cleft, away over to the right. Let me get a hold on that gun to steady me. That's all right. The rest's easy. I'll give you a hand across—that's right. Now we're there."

At the very foot of the cliff an unexplainable accident occurred. Dick's rifle went off with noise enough to wake the seven sleepers.

"Come on, Steve. We got to get out of here," he called to his partner, and began to run down the hill toward their cabin.

He covered ground so fast that the other could not keep up with him. From above there came the crack of a rifle, then another and another, as the men on the ridge sighted their prey. A spatter of bullets threw up the dirt around them. Dick felt a red-hot flame sting his leg, but, though he had been hit, to his surprise he was not checked.

Topping the brow of a little rise, he caught sight of the cabin, and, to his consternation, saw that smoke was pouring from the door and that within it was alight with flames.

"The beggars have set fire to it," he cried aloud.

So far as he could see, four men had been left below. They did not at first catch sight of him as he dodged forward in the shadows of the alders at the foot of the hill. Nor did they see him even when he stopped among the rocks at the rear, for their eyes were on Davis and their attention focused upon him.

He had come puffing to the brow of the hillock Gordon had already passed, when a shout from the ridge apprised those below of his presence. Cut off above and below, there was nothing left for Steve but a retreat down the road. He could not possibly advance in the face of four rifles, and he knew, too, that the best aid he could offer his friend was to deflect the attention of the watchers from him.

He fell back promptly, running from boulder to boulder in his retreat, pursued cautiously by the enemy. His ruse would have succeeded admirably, so far as Dick was concerned, except for that young man himself. He could not sit quiet and see his friend the focus of the fire.

Wherefore, it happened that the attackers of Davis were halted momentarily by a disconcerting fusillade from the rear. The "American devil" had come out into the open, and was dropping lead among them.

At this juncture a rider galloped into view from the river gorge along which wound the road. He pulled his jaded horse to a halt beside the old miner and leaped to the ground.

Without waiting an instant for their fire to cease, he ran straight forward toward the pursuing Mexicans.

As he came into the moonlight, Dick saw with surprise that the newcomer was Don Manuel Pesquiera. He was hatless, apparently too unarmed. But not for a second did this stop him as he sprinted forward.

Straight for the spitting rifles Don Manuel ran, face ablaze with anger. He had covered half the distance before the weapons wavered groundward.

"Don Manuel!" cried Sebastian, perturbed by this apparition flying through the night toward them.

Dick waited only long enough to make sure that hostilities had for the moment ceased against his friend before beginning his search for the tin box.

He quartered back and forth over the ground behind the burning house without result, circled it rapidly, his eyes alert to catch the shine of the box in the moonbeams, and examined the space among the rocks at the base of the hill. Nowhere did he see what he wanted.

"I'll have to take a whirl at the house. Some of them may have carried it back inside," he told himself.

As he stepped toward the door, Don Manuel came round the corner. At his heels were Steve and the four Mexicans who had but a few minutes before been trying industriously to exterminate the miner.

Don Manuel bowed punctiliously to Gordon.

"I beg to express my very great regrettance at this untimely attack," he said.

"Don't mention it, *don*. This business of chasing over the hills in the moonlight is first-class for the circulation of the blood, I expect. Most of us got quite a bit of exercise, first and last."

Dick spoke with light irony; but one distraught half of his attention was upon the burning house.

"Nevertheless, you will permeet me to regret, *senor*," returned the young Spaniard stiffly.

"Ce'tainly. You're naturally sore that you didn't get first crack at me. Don't blame you a bit," agreed Dick cheerfully but absently. "Funny thing is that one of your friends happened to send his message to my address, all right. Got me in the left laig, just before you butted in and spoiled their picnic so inconsiderate."

"You are then wounded, sir?"

"Not worth mentioning, *don*. Just a little accident. Wouldn't happen again in a thousand years. Never did see such poor shots as your valley lads. Say, will you excuse me just a minute? I got some awful important business to attend to."

"Most entirely, Senor Gordon."

"Thanks. Won't be a minute."

To Pesquiera's amazement, he dived through the door, from which smoke poured in clouds, and was at once lost to sight within.

"He is a madman," the Spaniard murmured.

"Or devil," added Sebastian significantly. "You will see, *senor*, he will come out safe and unharmed."

But he did not come out at all, though the minutes dragged themselves away one after another.

"I'm going after him," cried Davis, starting forward.

But Don Manuel flung strong arms about him, and threw the miner back into the hands of the Mexicans.

"Hold him," he cried in Spanish.

"Let me go. Let me go, I say!" cried the miner, struggling with those who detained him.

But Pesquiera had already gone to the rescue. He, too, plunged through the smoke. Blinded unable to breathe, he groped his way across the door lintel into the blazing hut.

The heat was intense. Red tongues of flame licked out from all sides toward him. But he would not give up, though he was gasping for breath and could not see through the dense smoke.

A sweep of wind brushed the smoke aside for an instant, and he saw the body of his enemy lying on the floor before him. He stooped, tried to pick it up, but was already too far gone himself.

Almost overcome, he sank to his knees beside Gordon. Close to the floor the air was still breathable. He filled his lungs, staggered to his feet, and tried to drag the unconscious man across the threshold with him.

A hundred fiery dragons sprang unleashed at him. The heat, the stifling smoke were more than flesh and blood could endure. He stumbled over a fallen chair, got up and plowed forward again, still with that dead weight in his arms; collapsed again, and yet once more pulled himself to his feet by the sheer strength of the dogged will in him.

So, at last, like a drunken man, he reeled into safety, the very hair and clothes of the man on fire from the inferno he had just left.

A score of eager hands were ready to relieve him of his burden, to support his lurching footsteps. Two of them were the strong brown hands of the woman he loved more than any other on earth, the woman who had galloped into sight just in time to see him come staggering from that furnace with the body of the man who was his hated rival. It was her soft hands that smothered the fire in his hair, that dragged the burning coat from his back.

He smiled wanly, murmured "Valencia," and fainted in her arms.

Gordon clutched in his stiffened fingers a tin box blistered by the heat.

CHAPTER XXIII

THE TIN BOX

Dick Gordon lay on a bed in a sunny south room at the Corbett place.

He was swathed in bandages, and had something the appearance of a relic of the Fourth of July, as our comic weeklies depict Young America the day after that glorious occasion. But, except for one thing which he had on his mind, the Coloradoan was as imperturbably gay as ever.

He had really been a good deal less injured than his rescuer; for, though a falling rafter had struck him down as he turned to leave the hut, this very accident had given him the benefit of such air as there had been in the cabin. Here and there he had been slightly burned, but he had not been forced to inhale smoke.

Wound in leg and all, the doctor had considered him out of danger long before he felt sure of Don Manuel.

The young Spaniard lay several days with his life despaired of. The most unremitting nursing on the part of his cousin alone pulled him through.

She would not give up; would not let his life slip away. And, in the end, she had won her hard fight. Don Manuel, too, was on the road to recovery.

While her cousin had been at the worst, Valencia Valdes saw the wounded Coloradoan only for a minute of two each day; but, with Pesquiera's recovery, she began to divide her time more equitably.

"I've been wishing I was the bad case," Dick told her whimsically when she came in to see him. "I'll bet I have a relapse so the head nurse won't always be in the other sick room."

"Manuel is my cousin, and he has been very, very ill," she answered in her low, sweet voice, the color in her olive cheeks renewed at his words.

The eyes of the Anglo-Saxon grew grave.

"How is Don Manuel to-night?"

"Better. Thank Heaven."

"That's what the doctor told me."

Dick propped himself on an elbow and looked directly at her, that affectionate smile of his on his face.

"Miss Valdes, do you know, ever since I've been well enough, I've been hoping that if one of us had to cross the Great Divide it would be me?"

Her troubled eyes studied him.

"Why do you say that?"

"Because it would seem more right that way. I came here and made all this trouble in the valley. I insulted him. I had in mind another hurt to him that we won't discuss just now. Then, when it comes to a showdown, he just naturally waltzes into Hades and saves my life for me at the risk of his own. No, ma'am, I sure couldn't have stood it if he had died."

"I'm glad you feel that way," she answered softly, her eyes dim.

"How else could I feel, and be a white man? I tell you, it makes me feel mean to think about that day I threw him in the water. Just because I'm a great big husky, about the size of two of him, I abused my strength and—"

"Just a moment," the girl smiled. "You are forgetting he struck you first."

"Oh, well! I reckon I could have stood that."

"Will you be willing to tell him how you feel about it?"

"Will I? Well, I guess yes."

The young woman's eyes were of starry radiance. "I'm so glad—so happy. I'm sure everything will come right, now."

He nodded, smiling.

"That's just the way I feel, Miss Valencia. They couldn't go wrong, after this—that is, they couldn't go clear wrong."

"I'm quite certain of that."

"I want to go on record as saying that Manuel Pesquiera is the gamest man I know. That isn't all. He's a thoroughbred on top of it. If I live to be a hundred I'll never be as fine a fellow. My hat's off to him."

There was a mist in her soft eyes as she poured a glass of ice water for him. "I'm so glad to hear you say that. He *is* such a splendid fellow."

He observed she was no longer wearing the solitaire and thought it might be to spare his feelings. So he took the subject as a hunter does a fence.

"I wish you all the joy in the world, Miss Valdes. I know you're going to be very happy. I've got my wedding present all picked out for you," he said audaciously.

She was busy tidying up his dresser, but he could see the color flame into her cheeks.

"You have a very vivid imagination, Mr. Gordon."

"Not necessary in this case," he assured her.

"You're quite sure of that, I suppose," she suggested with a touch of ironic mockery.

"I haven't read any announcement in the paper," he admitted.

"It is always safe to wait for that."

"Which is another way of saying that it is none of my business. But then you see it is." He offered no explanation of this statement, nor did he give her time to protest. "Now about that wedding present, Miss Valdes. It's in a tin box I had in the cabin before the fire. Can you tell me whether it was saved? My recollection is that I had it at the time the rafter put me to sleep. But of course I don't remember anything more till I found myself in bed here."

"A tin box? Yes; you had it in your hands when Manuel brought you out. They could hardly pry your fingers from it."

"Would you mind having that box brought to me, Miss Valdes? I want to be sure the present hasn't been injured by fire."

"Of course not. I don't just know where it is, but it must be somewhere about the place."

She was stepping toward the door, with that fine reaching grace of a fawn that distinguished her, when his voice stopped her. She stopped, delicate head poised and half turned, apparently waiting for further directions.

"Not just this minute, please. I've been lying here all day, with nobody but Steve. Finally he got so restless I had to turn him out to pasture. It wouldn't be right hospitable to send you away so soon. That box can wait till you have had all of me you can stand. What I need is good nursing, and I need it awful bad," he explained plaintively.

"Has Mrs. Corbett been neglecting you?"

"Mrs. Corbett—no!" he shouted with a spirit indomitable, but a voice still weak. "She's on earth merely to cook me chicken broth and custard. It's you that's been neglecting me."

The gleam of a strange fire was in her dark, bright eyes; in her cheeks the soft glow of beating color.

"And *my* business on earth is to fight you, is it not? But I can't do that till you are on your feet again, sir."

He gave her back her debonair smile.

"I'm not so sure of that. Women fight with the weapons of their sex—and often win, I'm told."

"You mean, perhaps, tears and appeals for pity. They are weapons I cannot use, sir. I had liefer lose."

"I dare say there are other weapons in your arsenal. I know you're too game to use those you've named."

"What others?" she asked quietly.

He let his eyes rest on her, sweep over her, and come back to the meeting with hers. But he did not name them. Instead, he came to another angle of the subject.

"You never know when you are licked, do you? Why don't you ask me to compromise this land grant business?"

"What sort of a compromise have you to offer, sir?" she said after a pause.

"Have your lawyers told you yet that you have no chance?"

"Would it be wise for me to admit I have none, before I go to discuss the terms of the treaty?" she asked, and put it so innocently that he acknowledged the hit with a grin.

"I thought that, if you knew you were going to lose, you might be easier to deal with. I'm such a fellow to want the whole thing in my bargains."

"If that's how you feel, I don't think I'll compromise."

"Well, I didn't really expect you would. I just mentioned it."

"It was very good of you. Now I think I'll go back to my cousin."

"If you must I'm coming over to his room as soon as the doc will let me, and as soon as he'll see me."

She gave him a sudden flash of happy eyes. "I hope you will. There must be no more trouble between him and you. There couldn't be after this, could there?"

He shook his head.

"Not if it takes two to make a quarrel. He can say what he wants to, make a door-mat out of me, go gunning after me till the cows come home, and I won't do a thing but be a delegate to a peace conference. No, ma'am. I'm through."

"You don't know how glad I am to hear it."

"Are you as anxious I should make up my quarrel with you as the ones with your friends?" he asked boldly.

The effrontery of this lean, stalwart young American—if effrontery it was, and no other name seemed to define it—surprised another dash of roses into the olive.

"The way to make up your quarrel with me is to make up those with my friends," she answered.

"All right. Suits me. I'll call those deputies off and send them home. Pablo and Sebastian will never go to the pen on my evidence. They're in the clear so far as I'm concerned."

She gave him both her hands. "Thank you. Thank you. I'm *so* glad."

The tears rose to her eyes. She bit her lip, turned and left the room.

He called after her:

"Please don't forget my tin box."

"I'll remember your precious box," she called back with a pretense of scorn.

He laughed to himself softly. There was sunshine in his eyes.

She had resolved to leave him to Mrs. Corbett in future, but within the hour she was back.

"I came about your tin box. Nobody seems to know where it is. Everybody remembers having seen it in your hands. I suppose we left it on the ground when we brought you to the house, but I can't find anybody that removed it. Perhaps some of my people have seen it. I'll send and ask them."

He smiled disconsolately.

"I may as well say good-bye to it."

"If you mean that my boys are thieves," she retorted hotly.

"I didn't say that, ma'am; but mebbe I did imply they wouldn't return that particular box, when they found what was in it. I shouldn't blame them if they didn't."

"I should. Very much. This merely shows you don't understand us at all, Mr. Gordon."

"I wish I had that box. It ce'tainly disarranges my plans to have it gone," he said irritably.

"I assure you I didn't take it."

"I don't lay it to you, though it would ce'tainly be to your advantage to take it," he laughed, already mollified.

"Will you please explain that?"

"All my claims of title to this land grant are in that box, Miss Valdes," he remarked placidly, as if it were a matter of no consequence.

She went white at his words.

"And it is lost—probably in the hands of my people. We must get it back."

"But you're on the other side of the fence," he reminded her gaily.

With dignity she turned on him.

"Do you think I want to beat you that way? Do you think I am a highwayman, or that I shall let my people be?"

"You make them draw the line between murder and robbery," he suggested pleasantly.

"I couldn't stop them from attacking you, but I can see they don't keep your papers—all the more, that it is to their interest and mine to keep them."

She said it with such fine girlish pride, her head thrown a little back, her eyes gleaming, scorn of his implied distrust in her very carriage. For long he joyfully carried the memory of it.

Surely, she was the rarest creature it had ever been his fortune to meet. Small wonder the gallant Spaniard Don Manuel loved her. Small wonder her people fed on her laughter, and were despondent at her frowns.

Dick Gordon was awake a good deal that night, for the pain and the fever were still with him; but the hours were short to him, full of joy and also of gloom. Shifting pictures of her filled the darkness. His imagination saw her in many moods, in many manners. And when from time to time he dropped into light sleep, it was to carry her into his dreams.

CHAPTER XXIV

DICK GORDON APOLOGIZES

Don Manuel was at first too spent a man even to wish to get well. As his cousin's nursing dragged him farther and farther back into this world from which he had so nearly slipped, he was content to lie still and take the goods the gods provided.

She was with him for the present. That sufficed. Whether he lived or died he did not care a hand's turn; but the while Fate flipped a coin to determine whether it should be life or death for him, he had Valencia's love as he feared he would never have it in case he recovered.

For these days she lived for him alone. Her every thought and desire had been for him. On this his soul fed, since he felt that, as they slipped back into the ordinary tide of life, she would withdraw herself gently but surely from him.

He had fought against the conviction that she loved his rival, the Colorado claimant to the valley. He had tried to persuade himself that her interest in the miner was natural under the circumstances and entirely independent of sentiment. But in the bottom of his heart such assurances did not convince.

"You will be able to sit up in a few days. It's wonderful how you have improved," she told him one day as she finished changing his pillow.

"Yes, I shall be well soon. You will be relieved of me," he said with a kind of gentle sadness.

"As if I wanted to be," she reproved softly, her hand smoothing down his hair.

"No. You're very good to me. You don't want to be rid of me. But it's best you should be. I have had all of you that's good for me, my cousin, unless I could have more than I dare hope."

She looked through the window at the sunlit warmth of the land, and, after a long time, said:

"Must we talk of that, Manuel?"

"No, *nina*—not if I am once sure. I have guessed; but I must be certain beyond the possibility of mistake. Is my guess right? That it can never be."

She turned dim eyes on him and nodded. A lump had risen to her throat that forbade speech.

"I can still say, dearest, that I am glad to have loved you," he answered cheerfully, after an instant's silence. "And I can promise that I shall trouble you no more. Shall we talk of something else?"

"There is one thing I should like to tell you first," she said with pretty timidity. "How proud I am that such a man could have loved me. You are the finest man I know. I must be a foolish girl not to—care for you—that way."

"No. A woman's heart goes where it must. If a man loses, he loses."

She choked over her words. "It doesn't seem fair. I promised. I wore your ring. I said that if you saved... him... I would marry you. Manuel, I... I'll keep faith if you'll take me and be content to wait for... that kind of love to grow."

"No, my cousin. I have wooed and lost. Why should you be bound by a pledge made at such a time? As your heart tells you to do, so you must do." He added after a pause: "It is this American, is it not?"

Again she nodded twice, not looking at him lest she see the pain in his eyes.

"I wish you joy, Valencia—a world full of it, so long as life lasts."

He took her fingers in his, and kissed them before he passed lightly to another subject:

"Have you heard anything yet of the tin box of Mr. Gordon's?"

She accepted the transition gratefully, for she was so moved she was afraid lest she break down.

"Not yet. It is strange, too, where it has gone. I have had inquiries made every where."

"For me, I hope it is never found. Why should you feel responsibility to search for these papers that will ruin you and your tenants?"

"If my men had not attacked and tried to murder him he

would still have his evidence. I seek only to put him in the position he was in before we injured him."

"You must judge for yourself, Valencia. But, if you don't mind, I shall continue to wish you failure in your search," he replied.

It was now that Jimmie Corbett came into the room to say that Mr. Gordon would like to call on Don Manuel, if the latter felt able to receive him.

Pesquiera did not glance at his cousin. He answered the boy at once.

"Tell Mr. Gordon I shall be very glad to see him," he said quietly.

Nor did he look at her after the boy had left the room, lest his gaze embarrass her, but gave his attention wholly to propping himself up on his elbow.

Dick stood a moment filling the doorway before he came limping into the room. From that point he bowed to Miss Valdes, then moved forward to the bed.

He did not offer to shake hands, but stood looking down at his rival, with an odd look of envy on his face. But it was the envy of a brave and generous man, who acknowledged victory to his foe.

"I give you best, Don Manuel," he finally said. "You've got me beat at every turn of the road. You saved my life again, and mighty near paid with your own. There ain't anything to say that will cover that, I reckon."

The Spaniard's eyes met his steadily, but Pesquiera did not

say a word. He was waiting to see what the other meant.

"You're a gamer man than I am, and a better one. All I can say is that I'm sorry and ashamed of myself for the way I treated you. If you still want to fight me, I'll stand up and give you a chance to pepper me. Anything you think right."

"If you put it so, sir, I have no choice but to join you in regrets and hopes of future amity."

"I can understand that you'd like to spill me over a ten-acre lot, and that you don't listen to my apologies with any joy," said the Coloradoan, smiling whimsically down at his former foe.

"I do not forget that the first offense was mine, *Senor Gordon*," the Spaniard answered.

Then came Jimmie Corbett again with a message for Miss Valdes.

"Pablo wants to see you, ma'am. Just rode over from the ranch. Says it's important."

The hands of the two men met in a strong grip as Valencia left the room, and so, too, did their steady gazes. Each of them knew that the other was his rival for the heart of the girl. Oddly enough, each thought the other was the successful suitor. But there was in each some quality of manliness that drew them together in spite of themselves.

Valencia found Pablo sitting on the porch. A rifle lay across his knees ready for emergencies. The deputies had ridden away to the other end of the valley that morning, but Menendez did not intend to be caught napping in case of their unexpected return.

Miss Valdes smiled. "You needn't be so careful, Pablo. I bring you good news—better than you deserve. Mr. Gordon has promised to drop the cases against you and Sebastian. Even if the officers arrest you, nothing can come of it except a trip to Santa Fe for a few days. If I were you I would give myself up. The rewards have been withdrawn, so it is not likely your friends will betray you."

"But, *Dona*, are you sure? Will this *Americano* keep his word? Is it certain they will not hold me in prison?"

"I tell you it is sure. Is that not enough? Did you find Mr. Gordon so ready to give you his word and break it when he was your prisoner?"

"True, *Dona*. He laughed at us and told us to kill him. He is a brave man."

"And brave men do not lie."

Pablo turned to his horse and took down from the horn of the saddle a gunny sack tied to it. This he opened. From it he drew a tin box that had been badly blistered with heat.

"It is *Senor* Gordon's tin box. After you carried him to the house here the other night I found it under a cottonwood. So I took it home with me. They are papers. Important—Is it not so?"

"Yes. I have been looking everywhere for them. You did right to bring them back to me."

"Perhaps they may help you win the land. Eh, *Dona*?"

"Perhaps. You know I offered a reward of twenty-five dollars for the box. It is yours. Buy some furniture with it when you and Juanita go to housekeeping."

"That is all past, alas, *Senorita*. Juanita looks down her nose when I am near. She does not speak to me."

"Foolish boy! That is a sign she thinks much of you. Tell her you did wrong to accuse her. Beg her to forgive you. Do not sulk, but love her and she will smile on you."

"But—this *Senor* Gordon?"

"All nonsense, Pablo. I have talked with Juanita. It is you she loves. Go to her and be good to her. She is back there in the milkhouse churning. But remember she is only a girl—so young, and motherless, too. It is the part of a man to be kind and generous and forbearing to a woman. He must be gentle—always gentle, if he would hold her love. Can you do that, Pablo? Or are you only a hot-headed, selfish, foolish boy?"

"I will try, *Dona*," he answered humbly. "For always have I love' her since she was such a little *muchacha*."

"Then go. Don't tell her I sent you. She must feel you have come because you could no longer stay away."

Pablo flashed his teeth in a smile of understanding and took the path that led round the house. He followed it to the sunken cellar that had been built for a milkhouse. Noiselessly he tiptoed down the steps and into the dark room. The plop-plop of a churn dasher told him Juanita was here even before his eyes could make her out in the darkness.

Presently he saw more clearly the slender figure bent a little wearily over the churn. Softly he trod forward. His hand went out and closed on the handle above hers. In startled surprise she turned.

"You—Pablo!" she cried faintly.

"I have so longed to see you—to come to you and tell you I was wrong, *nina*—Oh, you don't know how I have wanted to come. But my pride—my hard, foolish pride—it held me back. But no longer, heart of my heart, can I wait. Tell me that you forgive—that you will love me again—in spite of what I said and have done. I cannot get along without my little Juanita," he cried in the soft Spanish that was native to them both.

She was in his arms, crying softly, nestling close to him so that his love might enfold her more warmly. Always Juanita had been a soft, clinging child, happy only in an atmosphere of affection. She responded to caresses as a rose does to the sunlight. Pablo had been her first lover, the most constant of them all. She had relied upon him as a child does upon its mother. When he had left her in anger and not returned she had been miserably unhappy. Now all was well again, since Pablo had come back to her.

CHAPTER XXV

THE PRINCE CONSORT

Valencia returned to Don Manuel's room carrying a gunny sack. She found Dick Gordon sitting beside his rival's bed amiably discussing with him the respective values of the Silver Doctor and the Jock Scott for night fishing. Dick rose at her entrance to offer a chair.

She was all fire and animation. Her eyes sparkled, reflecting light as little wavelets of a sun-kissed lake.

"Supreme Court decision just come down in your favor?" asked the other claimant to the valley with genial irony.

"No, but—guess what I've got here."

"A new hat," hazarded Gordon, furrowing his brow in deep thought.

"Treason!" protested Manuel. "Does the lady live who would put her new hat in a gunny sack?"

"You may have three guesses, each of you," replied Miss Valdes, dimpling.

The miner guessed two guinea pigs, a million dollars, and a pair of tango slippers. Pesquiera went straight to the mark.

"A tin box," he said.

"Right, Manuel. Pablo brought it. He had just heard I was looking for the box—says he found it the night of the fire and took it home with him. His idea was that we might use the papers to help our fight."

"Good idea," agreed the Cripple Creek man, with twinkling eyes. "What are you going to do with the papers now you have them, Miss Valdes?"

"Going to give them to their owner," she replied, and swung the sack into his lap.

He took out a bunch of keys from his pocket, fitted one to the lock of the box, and threw up the lid. Carefully he looked the papers over.

"They are all here—every last one. I'm still lord of the Rio Chama Valley—unless my lawyers are fooling me mighty bad."

"It's a difference of opinion that makes horse races, *Senor*," retorted Manuel gaily from his pillows.

"I'll bet one of Mrs. Corbett's cookies there's no difference of opinion between my lawyers and those of Miss Valdes. What do you honestly think yourself about the legal end, ma'am?"

"I think that law and justice were divorced a good many years ago," she answered promptly.

"Which is another way of saying that you expect me to win out."

"By advice of counsel we decline to make any admissions, sir."

"You don't have to say a word. The facts do all the talking that is necessary." Gordon glanced in a business-like fashion over several papers. "This would be a fine time for friend Pablo to attack me again. Here are several of the original papers—deed of the grant, map of it with the first survey made, letters showing that old Moreno lived several years in the valley after your people were driven out at the time of the change in government. By the way, here's a rather interesting document. Like to look at it, Miss Valdes?"

He handed to her a paper done up in a blue cover after the fashion of modern legal pleadings. Valencia glanced it over. Her eye caught at a phrase which interested her and ran rapidly down the page.

"But—I don't understand what this means—unless—"

She looked up quickly at Gordon, an eager question in her face.

"It means what it says, though it's all wrapped up in dictionary words the way all law papers are."

Valencia passed the document to Pesquiera. "Read that, and tell me what you think it means, Manuel." Her face was flushed with excitement, and in her voice there was a suggestion of tremulousness.

The Spaniard read, and as he read his eyes, too, glowed.

"It means, my cousin, that you have to do with a very knightly foe. By this paper he relinquishes all claim, title and interest in the Moreno grant to Valencia Valdes, who he states to be in equity the rightful owner of same. Valencia, I congratulate you. But most of all I congratulate Mr. Gordon. Few men have the courage to make a gift of a half million acres of land merely because they have no moral title to it."

"Sho! I never did want the land, anyhow. I got interested in the scrap. That's all." The miner looked as embarrassed as if he had been caught stealing a box of cigars.

The young woman had gone from pink to white. The voice in which she spoke was low and unsteady.

"It's a splendid thing to do—the gift of a king. I don't know—that I can accept it—even for the sake of my people. I know now you would be fair to them. You wouldn't throw them out. You would give new deeds to those who have bought land, wouldn't you?"

"How are you going to keep from accepting it, Miss Valdes? That paper is a perfectly legal document."

She smiled faintly. "I could light a cigarette, Mr. Gordon, as you once did."

"Not a bit of use. I wired to Santa Fe by Steve to have that paper—the original of it—put on record this afternoon. By this time I expect you're the princess of the Rio Chama all right."

She still hesitated, the tide of feeling running full in her heart. It was all very well for this casual youth to make her a present of a half million acres of land in this debonair way, but she could not persuade herself to accept so munificent a gift.

"I don't know—I'll have to think—if you are the legal owner—"

"You're welching," he told her amiably. "I make a legal deed of conveyance because we are all agreed that my title isn't morally good. We're not a bunch of pettifoggers. All of us are aiming to get at what's right in settling this thing. You know what is right. So do I. So does Mr. Pesquiera. Enough said. All we have to do then is to act according to the best we know. Looks simple to me."

"Maybe it wouldn't look so simple if you were at the other end of the bargain, Mr. Gordon. To give is more blessed than to receive, you know."

"Sure. I understand that. I get the glory and do all the grandstanding. But you'll have to stand for it, I reckon."

"I'm going to think it over. Then I'll let you know what I can do." She looked at him sharply, a new angle of the situation coming home to her. "You meant to do this from the first, Mr. Gordon."

"Not quite from the first. After you had taken me to your ranch and I had seen how things stood between you and the folks in the valley I did. You've smoked me, ma'am. I'm a born grandstander." He laughed in amusement at himself. "I wanted to be it, the hero of the piece, the white-haired boy. But that wasn't the way it panned out. I was elected villain most unanimous, and came mighty near being put out of business a few times before I could make the public *sabe* I was only play acting. Funny how things work out. Right at the last when I've got the spotlight all trained for me to star and the music playing soft and low, Don Manuel here jumps in and takes the stage from me by rescuing the villain from a fiery furnace. I don't get any show," he complained whimsically.

Valencia smiled. "The action of the play has all revolved around you, anyhow. That ought to satisfy you. Without you there wouldn't have been any entertainment at all."

"I've had plenty of fun for my money. I'm not making any complaint at all. When a pretender invades a country to put the reigning queen out of business he has a license to expect a real warm welcome. Well, I got it."

Once again Jimmie Corbett appeared in the doorway, this time with a yellow envelope which he handed to Gordon.

Dick read the enclosed telegram and passed it to Pesquiera.

The Spaniard waved his hand and made a feeble attempt at a cheer.

"Am I to hear the good news?" Valencia asked.

"Read it, Mr. Pesquiera."

Manuel read:

> "Relinquishment of claim to Moreno grant in favor of Valencia Valdes filed ten minutes ago. Have you taken my advice in regard to consolidation?
>
> KATE UNDERWOOD."

"What does she mean about a consolidation?" asked Miss Valdes.

Dick flushed. "Oh, that was just something we were talking over—some foolishness or other, I reckon. Nothing to it. The important point is that the legal fight is over. You're now the owner of both the Valdes and the Moreno claims."

"*Le roi est mort! Vive la reine!*" cried Manuel gaily.

"I can't be said to have had a very peaceful reign. Wish you better luck, ma'am." He let his eyes rest drolly on the invalid for a moment. "And I hope when you take a prince consort to share the throne he'll meet all expectations—which I'm sure he will."

Dick shook hands with the bright-eyed flushing girl.

She laughed in the midst of her blushes. "*Gracias, senor!* I'll save your good wishes till they are needed."

"*Adios, Don* Manuel. See you to-morrow if you're up to it. I expect you've had enough excitement for one day."

"I'll let you know then whether I can accept your gift, Mr. Gordon," Valencia told him.

"That's all settled," he assured her as he left.

* * * * *

It was in the evening that he saw her again. Dick had stopped in the hall on the way to his room to examine a .303 Savage carbine he found propped against the wall. He had picked the weapon up when a voice above hailed him. He looked up. Valencia was leaning across the balustrade of the stairway.

"I want to talk with you, Mr. Gordon."

"Same here," he answered promptly. "I mean I want to talk with you. Let's take a walk."

"No. You're not up to a walk. We'll drive. My rig is outside."

Ten minutes later they were flying over the hard roads packed with rubble from decomposed sandstone. Neither of them spoke for some time. He was busy with the reins, and she was content to lean back and watch him. To her there was something very attractive about the set of his well-modeled head upon the broad shoulders. He had just been shaved, and the scent of the soap wafted to her a pleasant sense of intimacy with his masculinity. She could see the line above which the tiny white hairs grew thick on the bronzed cheeks. A strange delight stirred in her maiden heart, a joy in his physical well-being that longed for closer contact.

None of this reached the surface when she spoke at last.

"I can't let things go the way you have arranged them, Mr. Gordon. It isn't fair. After the way I and my people have treated you I can't be the object of such unlimited generosity at your hands."

"Justice," he suggested by way of substitution.

"No, generosity," she insisted. "Why should you be forced to give way to me? What have I done any more than you to earn all this?"

"Now you know we've all agreed—"

"Agreed!" she interrupted sharply. "We've taken it for granted that I had some sort of divine right. When I look into it I see that's silly. We're living in America, not in Spain of the seventeenth century. I've no right except what the law gives me."

"Well, the law's clear now. I'm tired of being shot at and starved and imprisoned and burned to make a Mexican holiday. I'm fed up with the excitement your friends have offered me. Honest, I'm glad to quit. I don't want the grant, anyhow. I'm a miner. We've just made a good strike in the Last Dollar. I'm going back to look after it."

"You can't make me believe anything of the kind, Mr. Gordon. I know you've made a strike, but you had made it before you ever came to the valley. Mr. Davis told me so. We simply couldn't drive you out. That's all humbug. You want me to have it—and I'm not going to take it. That's all there is to it, sir."

He smiled down upon her. "I never did see anyone so obstinate and so changeable. As long as I wanted the land you were going to have it; now I don't want it you won't take it. Isn't that just like a woman?"

"You know why I won't take it. From the very first you've played the better part. We've mistreated you in every way we could. Now you want to drown me in a lake of kindness. I just can't accept it. If you want to compromise on a fair business basis I'll do that."

"You've got a first-rate chance to be generous, too, Miss Valdes. I'm like a kid. I want to put this thing over my way so that I'll look big. Be a nice girl and let me have my own way. You know I said my wedding present was in that tin box. Don't spoil everything. Show me that you do think we're friends at last."

"We're friends—if you're sure you forgive me," she said shyly.

"Nothing in the world to forgive," he retorted cheerfully. "I've had the time of my life. Now I must go home and get to work."

"Yes," she agreed quietly, looking straight in front of her.

He drove in silence for a mile or two before he resumed the conversation.

"Of course I'll want to come back for the wedding if you send me an invitation. I think a good deal of the prince consort, you know. He's one man from the ground up."

"Yes?"

"He's the only man I know that's good enough for you. The more I see of him the better I like him. He's sure the gamest ever, a straight-up man if ever there was one."

"I'm glad of that." She flashed a little sidelong look at him and laughed tremulously. "It's good of you to pick me a husband you can endorse so heartily. Would you mind telling me his name—if it isn't a secret?"

"You know mighty well, but I reckon all girls play the game of making believe it isn't so for a while. All right. You don't have to admit it till the right time. But you'll send me a card, won't you?"

Her eyes, shyly daring, derided him. "That's no fair, Mr. Gordon. You go out of your way to pick a prince consort for me—a perfect paragon I'm given to understand—and then you expect me to say 'Thank you kindly, sir,' without even being told his name."

He smiled. "Oh, well, you can laugh at me all you like."

"But I'm not laughing at you," she corrected, her eyes dancing. "I'm trying to find out who this Admirable Crichton is. Surely I'm within my rights. This isn't Turkey, you know.

Perhaps I mayn't like him. Or, more important still, he may not like me."

"Go right ahead with your fun. Don't mind me."

"I don't believe you've got a prince consort for me at all. If you had you wouldn't dodge around like this."

At that instant he caught sight by chance of her ungloved left hand. Again he observed that the solitaire was missing. His eyes flashed to hers. A sudden hope was born in his heart. He drew the horse to a halt.

"Are you telling me that—? What about Don Manuel?" he demanded.

Now that the crisis was upon her, she would have evaded it if she could. Her long lashes fluttered to the hot cheeks.

"He is my cousin and my friend—the best friend I have," she answered in a low voice.

"No more than that?"

"No more." She lifted her eyes and tried to meet his boldly. "And now I really think you've been impudent enough, don't you?"

He imprisoned her hands in his. "If it isn't Don Manuel who is it?"

She knew her eyes had failed her, that they had told him too much. An agony of shyness drenched her from head to foot, but there was no escape from his masterful insistence.

"Will you let me go... please?"

"No—not till you tell me that you love me, Valencia, not till you've made me the happiest man alive."

"But..."

He plunged forward, an insurgent hope shaking his imperturbability.

"Is it yes, dear? Don't keep me waiting. Do I win or lose, Valencia?"

Bravely her eyes lifted to his. "I love you with all my heart and soul. I always have from the first. I always shall as long as life lasts," she murmured.

Swept away by the abandon of her adorable confession, he caught her in his arms and drew her to him. Close as breathing he held her, her heart beating against his like a fluttering bird. A delicious faintness overcame her. She lay in his embrace, wonderfully content.

The dewy eyes lifted again to his. Of their own volition almost their lips met for the first kiss.

THE END

Choose from Thousands of 1stWorldLibrary Classics By

A. M. Barnard
Ada Leverson
Adolphus William Ward
Aesop
Agatha Christie
Alexander Aaronsohn
Alexander Kielland
Alexandre Dumas
Alfred Gatty
Alfred Ollivant
Alice Duer Miller
Alice Turner Curtis
Alice Dunbar
Allen Chapman
Alleyne Ireland
Ambrose Bierce
Amelia E. Barr
Amory H. Bradford
Andrew Lang
Andrew McFarland Davis
Andy Adams
Angela Brazil
Anna Alice Chapin
Anna Sewell
Annie Besant
Annie Hamilton Donnell
Annie Payson Call
Annie Roe Carr
Annonaymous
Anton Chekhov
Archibald Lee Fletcher
Arnold Bennett
Arthur C. Benson
Arthur Conan Doyle
Arthur M. Winfield
Arthur Ransome
Arthur Schnitzler
Arthur Train
Atticus
B.H. Baden-Powell
B. M. Bower
B. C. Chatterjee
Baroness Emmuska Orczy
Baroness Orczy
Basil King
Bayard Taylor
Ben Macomber
Bertha Muzzy Bower
Bjornstjerne Bjornson

Booth Tarkington
Boyd Cable
Bram Stoker
C. Collodi
C. E. Orr
C. M. Ingleby
Carolyn Wells
Catherine Parr Traill
Charles A. Eastman
Charles Amory Beach
Charles Dickens
Charles Dudley Warner
Charles Farrar Browne
Charles Ives
Charles Kingsley
Charles Klein
Charles Hanson Towne
Charles Lathrop Pack
Charles Romyn Dake
Charles Whibley
Charles Willing Beale
Charlotte M. Braeme
Charlotte M. Yonge
Charlotte Perkins Stetson
Clair W. Hayes
Clarence Day Jr.
Clarence E. Mulford
Clemence Housman
Confucius
Coningsby Dawson
Cornelis DeWitt Wilcox
Cyril Burleigh
D. H. Lawrence
Daniel Defoe
David Garnett
Dinah Craik
Don Carlos Janes
Donald Keyhoe
Dorothy Kilner
Dougan Clark
Douglas Fairbanks
E. Nesbit
E. P. Roe
E. Phillips Oppenheim
E. S. Brooks
Earl Barnes
Edgar Rice Burroughs
Edith Van Dyne
Edith Wharton

Edward Everett Hale
Edward J. O'Biren
Edward S. Ellis
Edwin L. Arnold
Eleanor Atkins
Eleanor Hallowell Abbott
Eliot Gregory
Elizabeth Gaskell
Elizabeth McCracken
Elizabeth Von Arnim
Ellem Key
Emerson Hough
Emilie F. Carlen
Emily Bronte
Emily Dickinson
Enid Bagnold
Enilor Macartney Lane
Erasmus W. Jones
Ernie Howard Pie
Ethel May Dell
Ethel Turner
Ethel Watts Mumford
Eugene Sue
Eugenie Foa
Eugene Wood
Eustace Hale Ball
Evelyn Everett-green
Everard Cotes
F. H. Cheley
F. J. Cross
F. Marion Crawford
Fannie E. Newberry
Federick Austin Ogg
Ferdinand Ossendowski
Fergus Hume
Florence A. Kilpatrick
Fremont B. Deering
Francis Bacon
Francis Darwin
Frances Hodgson Burnett
Frances Parkinson Keyes
Frank Gee Patchin
Frank Harris
Frank Jewett Mather
Frank L. Packard
Frank V. Webster
Frederic Stewart Isham
Frederick Trevor Hill
Frederick Winslow Taylor

Friedrich Kerst
Friedrich Nietzsche
Fyodor Dostoyevsky
G.A. Henty
G.K. Chesterton
Gabrielle E. Jackson
Garrett P. Serviss
Gaston Leroux
George A. Warren
George Ade
Geroge Bernard Shaw
George Cary Eggleston
George Durston
George Ebers
George Eliot
George Gissing
George MacDonald
George Meredith
George Orwell
George Sylvester Viereck
George Tucker
George W. Cable
George Wharton James
Gertrude Atherton
Gordon Casserly
Grace E. King
Grace Gallatin
Grace Greenwood
Grant Allen
Guillermo A. Sherwell
Gulielma Zollinger
Gustav Flaubert
H. A. Cody
H. B. Irving
H.C. Bailey
H. G. Wells
H. H. Munro
H. Irving Hancock
H. R. Naylor
H. Rider Haggard
H. W. C. Davis
Haldeman Julius
Hall Caine
Hamilton Wright Mabie
Hans Christian Andersen
Harold Avery
Harold McGrath
Harriet Beecher Stowe
Harry Castlemon
Harry Coghill
Harry Houidini

Hayden Carruth
Helent Hunt Jackson
Helen Nicolay
Hendrik Conscience
Hendy David Thoreau
Henri Barbusse
Henrik Ibsen
Henry Adams
Henry Ford
Henry Frost
Henry James
Henry Jones Ford
Henry Seton Merriman
Henry W Longfellow
Herbert A. Giles
Herbert Carter
Herbert N. Casson
Herman Hesse
Hildegard G. Frey
Homer
Honore De Balzac
Horace B. Day
Horace Walpole
Horatio Alger Jr.
Howard Pyle
Howard R. Garis
Hugh Lofting
Hugh Walpole
Humphry Ward
Ian Maclaren
Inez Haynes Gillmore
Irving Bacheller
Isabel Cecilia Williams
Isabel Hornibrook
Israel Abrahams
Ivan Turgenev
J.G.Austin
J. Henri Fabre
J. M. Barrie
J. M. Walsh
J. Macdonald Oxley
J. R. Miller
J. S. Fletcher
J. S. Knowles
J. Storer Clouston
J. W. Duffield
Jack London
Jacob Abbott
James Allen
James Andrews
James Baldwin

James Branch Cabell
James DeMille
James Joyce
James Lane Allen
James Lane Allen
James Oliver Curwood
James Oppenheim
James Otis
James R. Driscoll
Jane Abbott
Jane Austen
Jane L. Stewart
Janet Aldridge
Jens Peter Jacobsen
Jerome K. Jerome
Jessie Graham Flower
John Buchan
John Burroughs
John Cournos
John F. Kennedy
John Gay
John Glasworthy
John Habberton
John Joy Bell
John Kendrick Bangs
John Milton
John Philip Sousa
John Taintor Foote
Jonas Lauritz Idemil Lie
Jonathan Swift
Joseph A. Altsheler
Joseph Carey
Joseph Conrad
Joseph E. Badger Jr
Joseph Hergesheimer
Joseph Jacobs
Jules Vernes
Julian Hawthrone
Julie A Lippmann
Justin Huntly McCarthy
Kakuzo Okakura
Karle Wilson Baker
Kate Chopin
Kenneth Grahame
Kenneth McGaffey
Kate Langley Bosher
Kate Langley Bosher
Katherine Cecil Thurston
Katherine Stokes
L. A. Abbot
L. T. Meade

L. Frank Baum	Paul G. Tomlinson	T. S. Arthur
Latta Griswold	Paul Severing	The Princess Der Ling
Laura Dent Crane	Percy Brebner	Thomas A. Janvier
Laura Lee Hope	Percy Keese Fitzhugh	Thomas A Kempis
Laurence Housman	Peter B. Kyne	Thomas Anderton
Lawrence Beasley	Plato	Thomas Bailey Aldrich
Leo Tolstoy	Quincy Allen	Thomas Bulfinch
Leonid Andreyev	R. Derby Holmes	Thomas De Quincey
Lewis Carroll	R. L. Stevenson	Thomas Dixon
Lewis Sperry Chafer	R. S. Ball	Thomas H. Huxley
Lilian Bell	Rabindranath Tagore	Thomas Hardy
Lloyd Osbourne	Rahul Alvares	Thomas More
Louis Hughes	Ralph Bonehill	Thornton W. Burgess
Louis Joseph Vance	Ralph Henry Barbour	U. S. Grant
Louis Tracy	Ralph Victor	Upton Sinclair
Louisa May Alcott	Ralph Waldo Emmerson	Valentine Williams
Lucy Fitch Perkins	Rene Descartes	Various Authors
Lucy Maud Montgomery	Ray Cummings	Vaughan Kester
Luther Benson	Rex Beach	Victor Appleton
Lydia Miller Middleton	Rex E. Beach	Victor G. Durham
Lyndon Orr	Richard Harding Davis	Victoria Cross
M. Corvus	Richard Jefferies	Virginia Woolf
M. H. Adams	Richard Le Gallienne	Wadsworth Camp
Margaret E. Sangster	Robert Barr	Walter Camp
Margret Howth	Robert Frost	Walter Scott
Margaret Vandercook	Robert Gordon Anderson	Washington Irving
Margaret W. Hungerford	Robert L. Drake	Wilbur Lawton
Margret Penrose	Robert Lansing	Wilkie Collins
Maria Edgeworth	Robert Lynd	Willa Cather
Maria Thompson Daviess	Robert Michael Ballantyne	Willard F. Baker
Mariano Azuela	Robert W. Chambers	William Dean Howells
Marion Polk Angellotti	Rosa Nouchette Carey	William le Queux
Mark Overton	Rudyard Kipling	W. Makepeace Thackeray
Mark Twain	Saint Augustine	William W. Walter
Mary Austin	Samuel B. Allison	William Shakespeare
Mary Catherine Crowley	Samuel Hopkins Adams	Winston Churchill
Mary Cole	Sarah Bernhardt	Yei Theodora Ozaki
Mary Hastings Bradley	Sarah C. Hallowell	Yogi Ramacharaka
Mary Roberts Rinehart	Selma Lagerlof	Young E. Allison
Mary Rowlandson	Sherwood Anderson	Zane Grey
M. Wollstonecraft Shelley	Sigmund Freud	
Maud Lindsay	Standish O'Grady	
Max Beerbohm	Stanley Weyman	
Myra Kelly	Stella Benson	
Nathaniel Hawthrone	Stella M. Francis	
Nicolo Machiavelli	Stephen Crane	
O. F. Walton	Stewart Edward White	
Oscar Wilde	Stijn Streuvels	
Owen Johnson	Swami Abhedananda	
P.G. Wodehouse	Swami Parmananda	
Paul and Mabel Thorne	T. S. Ackland